Saracen Tales

Giuseppe Bonaviri

Translated by
Barbara De Marco

BORDIGHERA

Library of Congress Cataloguing-in-Publication Data

Bonaviri, Giuseppe, 1924–
[Novelle saracene. English]
Saracen tales / Giuseppe Bonaviri ; translated by Barbara De
Marco.
  p. cm. – (Crossings ; 16)
Includes bibliographical references.
ISBN 1-884419-76-3 (alk. paper)
I. De Marco, Barbara. II. Title.

PQ4862.O496N6813 2006
853'.91—dc22

2006043025

The publication of this volume has been made possible through the generous support of the Fondazione Giuseppe Bonaviri, in the town of Minèo, Giuseppe Bonaviri's birthplace.

Printed in the United States.

Published by
BORDIGHERA PRESS
John D. Calandra Italian American Institute
25 W. 43rd Street, 17th Floor
New York, NY 10036

CROSSINGS 16
ISBN 1-884419-76-3

Table of Contents

❖

Saracen Tales

Jesus and Giufà

Profane Stories

Fables

❖

Introduction

Franco Zangrilli

When the discipline of Comparative Literature began to come into its own in the United States in the early seventies, the art of translation suddenly became a topic of intense debate. It was discussed by literary critics of differing backgrounds and disciplines, whose approaches were sometimes original, sometimes superficial, and sometimes merely contained ideas that were both captious and confused. It was a topic among semiologists, philosophers, translators, writers, and students of esthetics, who espoused provocative theories. One had the impression there was no one who did not have his or her own theory of literary translation. At the same time, in many American universities, from Columbia to Yale to New York University, newly created departments, dedicated exclusively to translation, sponsored seminars, symposia, and conferences on the theme.

During the same period, presentations of literary translations were scheduled in numerous cities in the United States, from New York to Los Angeles, in cultural centers and associations, in prestigious lecture halls and libraries. At these events, the author, the translator, and the general public gathered to discuss the merits of new translations.

Often the authors of the works under discussion were from Latin America, not only because they were writers of quality, but also because their works were easily marketable, their books sold well, even without recourse to sophisticated marketing strategies. As a result, chain bookstores, large and small, dedicated rows of shelves, store windows, and other places of prominence to the translated works of these authors. Only with difficulty could one find translated works of contemporary Italian writers of the level of Pirandello – the exceptions were Italo Calvino and Umberto Eco, who are extremely popular among American readers, in no small part because they have been embraced as representatives of postmodernism.

Even now, the theme of "the translator and the translated" continues to be a matter of debate. Certainly, it is a topic of great relevance to the study of Giuseppe Bonaviri, whose considerable body of work has been translated in part. According to the testimony of those who have translated him into English, French, and Russian, among other languages, Bonaviri is not an easy writer to translate.

Anyone who has ever attempted to translate a literary text – whether novel, short story, poetry, or drama – knows that translation presents a multitude of problems, difficulties, and challenges. Obviously, translating a text by Alberto Moravia, who uses a simple, even pedestrian, style of language, presents fewer problems than translating a work by Carlo Emilio Gadda, Tommaso Landolfi, or Giuseppe Bonaviri, each of whom writes in a complex and sophisticated language, a studied language, at once scientific and literary, and each of whom tends to write in a mixture of languages and expressive means. Translation is a difficult art – bordering at times on the mechanical and monotonous, but also at times capable of bringing to literary life the seemingly untranslatable. In the opinion of some scholars, everything can be translated, if translation is understood to mean simply recreating a text in a second language while remaining faithful to the message in the original language. But as a creative art, translation requires more, as other critics and translators maintain – among them, Tommaso Landolfi, who produced Italian translations of several Russian writers (see his *Gogol in Rome* [Florence: Vallecchi Editore, 1971]). Theorists agree that the process of translation, when undertaken by a person who knows both languages well, can become a process of invention.

As a case in point, when Gregory Rabassa's translation of Gabriel Garcia Marquez' masterpiece, *One Hundred Years of Solitude* (New York: Harper & Row, 1970), was presented in New York, critics declared that on several levels, Rabassa had re-created the novel – especially on the formal level, which, as we know, often determines the contents, and therefore, the message of the novel. Here one may recall the saying "traduttore traditore." A translator who sets out to translate a literary text must make some basic choices: either the form and the content of the text must be respected absolutely, or the text must be altered so as to render it more accessible to a new reading public.

On occasion, and even among translators themselves, there arise bitter disagreements, polemics, controversies. There are those who are convinced that certain writers – James Joyce, for example – , simply cannot be translated. There are those who are of the opinion that the works of certain writers or poets are diminished in translation – English translations of Leopardi are a case in point. There are those who feel that certain other writers or poets are in fact improved by translation – Pirandello in English, for example – , and perhaps this is the case for works that are written in a kind of spoken idiom. There are still others who hold to the idea that many post-modern writers (among them, Umberto Eco, Nicolò Ammaniti, Alessandro Baricco) deliberately employ a journalistic style in their writing, so as to be more easily translated into English, a language which enjoys an almost universal vogue.

When I edited the volume entitled *Il mitico muro. Lettere di scrittori italiani a un traduttore russo: Lev Verscinen* (Isernia – Venafro: Eva Edizioni, 2001), I realized that some of the choices that the translator has to make, if taken to their logical conclusion, may cause considerable difficulty, and often the results may not be appreciated by the author. The author of the text and the translator may disagree bitterly over how to translate a word, a phrase, a scene. Italo Calvino, finding himself at odds with Verscinen over his translation of one of Calvino's short stories, went so far as to prohibit the publication of the translation. Several letters testify that Verscinen repeatedly asked Giuseppe Bonaviri for a more detailed clarification of the author's style, the function of certain stylistic and lexical choices, the meaning of this or that word, the syntax of a lengthy sentence, a given image, and so on.

Having myself produced translations (from Spanish into Italian and from English into Italian), including translations of some of Bonaviri's poetry (see *Uno scrittore come Bonaviri*, Rome: Edizioni della Cometa, 1995), I immediately realized that English versions of Bonaviri's work would require an expert American translator.

The first translator of Bonaviri in America was Umberto Mariani, who translated the first two chapters of the novel *La divina foresta*, a selection from the novel *Notti sull'altura*, three poems from *Il dire celeste* ("My Father," "The Tailor Al-Aggiag," "Andromeda"), the tale "La fidanzata di Gesù" ("Jesus' Girl"), and four poems from the collection *O corpo sospiroso* ("Holy Thursday," "Good Friday," "The Lamplighter," "The Three Children"). All of these translations, with facing Italian text, appeared in the Special issue on Giuseppe Bonaviri published in the journal *La Fusta* (Dept. of Italian, Rutgers University), vol. VI, nos. 1-2 (Spring-Fall 1981), pp. 220-278. Mariani then translated, with great intelligence and delicacy, one of the most characteristic and successful of Bonaviri's works, the novel *Dolcissimo* (New York: Italica Press, 1990).

The second American translator of Bonaviri was Giovanni Bussino, who produced a brilliant translation of the novel *Notti sull'altura* (*Nights on the Heights* [New York: Peter Lang, 1990]).

Anna Paolucci translated four stories from the *Novelle Saracene* ("Jesus and Jewfas," "The Parrot," "Jesus' Brother," "The Little Green Horse"), which appeared in an anthology entitled *Contemporary Italian Fiction: Luigi Pirandello, Mario Pomilio, Giuseppe Bonaviri* (ed. Franco Zangrilli; New York: Griffon House Publications, 1988).

The American publishing house Bordighera Press now presents a beautiful translation by Barbara De Marco of the entire collection of tales in Bonaviri's *Novelle Saracene* (Milan: Rizzoli, 1980). As a translator, she has worked with the patience of a monk, re-creating in English the lyrical tones, the linguistic nuances, and even the neologisms of Bonaviri's style. As if by magic, she renders accessible to an audience of readers in English a work that is perhaps the most mythical and poetic of Bonaviri's vast corpus of writings.

The co-mingling of myths, archetypes, and symbols of diverse and even clashing cultures is a recurring feature of Bonaviri's work, all the more strikingly intense in the fables he has created around the Saracen Jesus. Bonaviri is a myth-maker, looking simultaneously to the historical past and to the future, to arrive at the a-historical, at cosmic universality. In his works, traditional myths become transformed or "contaminated" in an inventive fashion; they are reordered, reversed, rewritten, to join together opposing time and space, to fuse cultures and civilizations from different times, and even to express their affirmation and negation. Bonaviri seems, in fact, to prefer the imaginative process of re-creating a myth – be it Christian, folkloric, or literary in origin. He is interested above all in exploring the known and the unknown, the real and the unreal, the infinitely large and the infinitesimally small; he prefers to view mankind in relation to the cosmos, considering differing types of religions, from the pantheistic to the Franciscan evangelical tradition, from the arcane wisdom advocated by the eccentric Father Onorio in *Dolcissimo* to the more cosmic view preached by the Buddhist monk in *Dottor Bilob*. The works of Bonaviri (whether poetry, short stories, or novels) frequently reveal the influence of the Bible, of the Qur'an, and of Eastern religious texts (see, for example, *È un rosseggiar di peschi e d'albicocchi*, or *O corpo sospiroso*, or *Il dire celeste*).

In the *Novelle Saracene*, a work composed of twenty-six tales, the author reveals himself to be a man of wisdom and an inventor of tales, one who is particularly given to re-working religious myths, making use of them to enrich his cosmic vision of reality.

The imaginative reinterpretations of Bonaviri begin with, and linger over, the figure of the mother. She is often presented with attributes that are noble, angelic, divine; at the same time she is transformed into a female image that is folkloric, mythical, universal.

In "The Child Mother," an enchanting tale that combines myth and autobiography, Bonaviri's imagination, adept at transforming the simplest personal memory into ineffable mystery, narrates the events of his mother's girlhood. He writes in the voice of his mother, now so aged as to have lost "the divine loving memory of childhood" and forgotten the "garlands of fables" that she once knew. The affection of Bonaviri for his octogenarian mother finds a fresh lyrical vein of expression.

Gradually there comes to life before our eyes the picture of a vibrant young girl, full of restless energy, always in motion, always immersed in an environment filled with wonders that stimulate her sensibility and intellectual curiosity. She rises in the middle of the night to help her father bake bread, an image filled with religious symbolism, as occurs in certain descriptions written by Ignacio Silone. Once her work is finished, instead of going to bed, she wanders through the countryside, absorbed in the early morning silence, waking the other young girls, leading them in their games, playing tricks on the villagers, taking young Maruzzedda into her care, playing at being mommy to a doll made of stone that she takes everywhere with her.

Bonaviri, gazing into the mirror of this restless mother, recognizes himself, sees that it is from her that he derives his own restlessness, and that he becomes calm by simply listening to her, just as she used to quiet down as soon as the old Centamore sisters would start to tell her stories.

Here then is a first realization of the archetypal image of the mother-storyteller, followed by an accumulation of events and imaginative allusions that identify the figure of the mother with the marvelous and mysterious process of artistic creation. These events and allusions create an ambiguous figure of child and crone, of innocent instincts and accumulated wisdom, of utopian yearnings and memory.

In the remainder of the *Novelle*, the most frequent maternal image is that of the "mother of sorrows." Aggrieved by the injustices committed against her children, and by being abandoned and forgotten by them, her sighs and tears are the signs of her affliction, and even more, are symbols of the burden of her existence.

The tale "Jesus and Giufà" presents two versions of the sorrowing mother: Mary and Magdalene. Mary, the mother of Jesus, ashamed of not knowing the identity of the father of her child, first abandons him at birth in a cave, then searches desperately for him. She finds him at last, but discovers he is being persecuted by Frederick II. Jesus becomes ill, and Mary must entrust him to the care of her sister, Magdalene. Magdalene, whose son Giufà is a source of constant sorrow, grieves as well for her nephew Jesus, suffering from a serious illness and from persecution by the Christian king, Frederick II.

In "The Death of Jesus," the sorrowful mother faces the ultimate test, the death of her son. Jesus is arrested by Frederick's guards, along with Giufà and Orlando. Mary runs to her son: "Child of the black forehead, / My ardent beauty, / Dawn in the star's ray, / Oh, who tortures and afflicts you?" (49). At the end of the story, not only the three Marys but an entire chorus of "Saracen mothers" lament the loss of their children, represented by the trinity Jesus, Giufà, and Orlando.

Only on rare occasions does the image of the unfortunate mother of sorrows alternate with a vision of the mother that is not entirely alien to the Christian version. This occurs in "The Resurrection of Giufà," in which Giufà frees the villagers from Frederick II's oppression and they make him king of Minaw (Minèo). But the image that prevails in the entire collection of tales is that of the mother who suffers from human malevolence.

In "The Bird with the Blue Feathers" we are presented with the figure of a "Queen Mother who has two children, her son Corradino and her stepson Manfredo. The two set out together to find the bird with the blue feathers, in the hopes of winning the reward promised by their father, King Frederick. Corradino finds the bird, whereupon he is killed by his "heartless brother, son of a different mother" (152), who then brings the bird to King Frederick, from whom he receives the prize. The "Queen Mother" is sorely afflicted by the death of her son, and when she learns of the tragic deception, she dies of sorrow, as much for the crime committed by her stepson as for the loss of her son: "The Queen did nothing but cry, her pain was so great. She fell sick and died" (154).

Another mother in these tales is "Holy Mother Church," an evil stepmother who represents corruption, vice, and all kinds of evil. She makes use of her un-Christian servants to persecute the underground church, made up of the small community of Saracens, consisting of Jesus, his followers, friends, and the faithful, whose actions are imbued (paradoxically) with a Franciscan evangelical spirit. The Pope, for example, unhappy that Jesus has assembled a traveling band, playing their instruments in an attempt to lift the spirits of the sad people of Minaw, "thought to call King Frederick" and to have him arrest Jesus, and so "The army of the Normans came – horses, knights with swords and resounding guns. Our island was crowded with them. The earth trembled" (340–41).

Bonaviri, like Pirandello, is a writer who is a non-believer; nonetheless, both writers invest their work with a religious sense of reality, a Franciscan spirit of life, and they both criticize harshly the world of the Catholic church and its representatives. In these tales, Bonaviri's criticisms of the Church show a Pirandellian humor. Like Pirandello, in *I vecchi e i giovani* and other works, Bonaviri makes use of satire, irony, and sarcasm, the paradoxical, ridiculous, and comical – in short, all the tools of humor, understood in its widest and its narrowest sense, are brought into play to pillory the workings of powerful men – and not only those of the Catholic church.

In "The White Girl Named Maria," the mother of Jesus, having refused the offer of marriage from Herod's son, is condemned to death, along with her parents, whereupon, they all disappear in a wisp of smoke: "Everyone was frightened, realizing that Maria was the mother of Jesus. The knights remained with their swords aloft. The executioner fell dead upon the scaffold. The faithful, lay people and religious, went out, dispersed through dark caves, into the world" (107).

Whether the tale is Bonaviri's own invention or the continuation of a tradition, the plot of the *Novelle Saracene* always tends to represent the mythical world of the maternal. In "Jesus on the Moon," Jesus recounts the origin of the cosmos to the Saracen mothers, an image that Bonaviri uses to suggest that everything is born of female seeds – the air, time, even God ("dio-femmina"), the great mother in whom being has its origins.

In every tale we find the mythical image of the mother, as protector, counsel, and guide, always ready to attend to the needs of others (this is true even if the figure is a servant woman, as in the tale "Lady Catherine").

Bonaviri's imaginings in these tales do not run to the erotic or sexual, which are seen only as the necessary antecedent to maternity, the true center of the narrator's insight. Even when the pregnancy is unwanted, as happens to Maria in "Jesus and Giufà," or when it is the consequence of violence, as happens to Tamàr, violated by King Herod, in "The Boy with the Little Golden Horns," the maternal sentiments felt by the unfortunate girl for her children do not alter. Thus, Bonaviri's narrative imagination portrays the biological and the non-biological mother in the same light. In "Jesus' Brother," Maria is the biological mother of the mystically conceived Jesus and the biological mother of Giovannipaolo, born of her marriage with mastro Antonio; she also becomes the stepmother of Antonio's two children, Salvatore and Pina: "That poor thing, Maria of Jesus, truly loved the two children. She treated them like a mother who gives her breasts to suck, and protects them from the dark night" (84), and her stepchildren respond wonderfully to her care. Elsewhere, Bonaviri presents us with other versions of the adoptive mother, as in the second part of the story of "The Lover Made of Honey." The miller's wife in "The Twins as White as Lilies" finds two children and adopts them; by contrast, the Queen in "The Lover Made of Honey" buys Sion and adopts him as her son. She becomes a trifle too possessive, for when Granata asks to marry him, the Queen is not at all inclined to let him go, and she allows him to sleep with his wife only after administering a sleeping draught that causes him to embark on the waters of sleep. Only later does the Queen release these possessive feelings for her son, and from an overly protective mother she becomes a kindly mother-in-law.

The mother-in-law in "The Twins as White as Lilies," on the other hand, remains evil. The witch Zebaide does not approve of the marriage of her son Giuseppe to Proserpina. No sooner does Giuseppe leave his home to go to battle, along with the other knights, leaving behind his pregnant wife, than Zebaide prepares a "dark command" against her daughter-in-law. After Proserpina gives birth, Zebaide, with the help of the midwife, arranges for the disappearance of the two children. When their mother asks to see her babies, Zebaide tells her that she has given birth to two lambs, and then gives orders to her servant to destroy the newborn children. However, at the end of the tale, Zebaide's son, having meanwhile become king, discovers the truth and orders his mother killed. The outcome of this story—that of the son who kills his mother or stepmother – is, according to Bruno Bettelheim, extremely rare in the world of folktales (see his *Il mondo incantato: Uso, importanza e significati psicanalitici delle fiabe* [Milan: Feltrinelli, 1979], p. 235; Italian translation of *The Uses of Enchantment: The Meaning and Importance of Fairy Tales* [New York: Vintage Books, 1977]).

Among the maternal figures to whom the fertile imagination of Bonaviri gives birth, is that of the animal imbued with religious symbolism, that is, the image of the animal-mother who demonstrates the maternal qualities of nurturing and protecting.

This, for example, is the lamb who nurtures Jesus in "Jesus and Giufà," the she-goat in "The Twins as White as Lilies," and the cow in "Lady Catherine," whose milk comes to represent a spiritual nourishment as well: "every two days, a cow who understood the speech of humans came up to Catherine, and offered her full teats" (111).

Students of primitive societies tell us that the figure of the mother is connected to the figure of death, not a death that leads to the kingdom of God, but a death that leads back to the original state of chaos, to an origin of the universe not unlike the original embyronic state in the maternal womb. Thus, death becomes assimilated to the myth of the eternal return, a return to the obscurity of chaos. According to Mircea Eliade, "the return to the womb corresponds to the reversion of the Universe to the 'chaotic' or embryonic state ... The return to the womb is signified either by the neophyte's seclusion in a hut, or by his being symbolically swallowed by a monster" (Myth and Reality [New York: Harper & Row, 1963], p. 80). The mythic and inventive imagination of Bonaviri develops this aspect of the maternal figure in "Jesus' Brother," in "The Tailor's Son," and in "Jesus on the Moon."

Set in the author's native land, the Novelle Saracene create an image of a maternal Sicily, both historical and fabulous, with a centuries'-old history of successive cultural layers: the ancient Siculi, the Greeks, Romans, Arabs, Normans, French, and Spanish. Thus we are presented with a Sicily that is the mother of cultures, a Sicilian land that nurtures and gives life, a land which, in the course of centuries, has encountered many different religions. In "The Resurrection of Giufà," Giufà is himself reborn from the womb of the mother earth, after having been asleep for many years: "Everyone watched him come up from out of the earth" (19). The farmer and his wife, who are the protagonists of "The Animals," have a visceral relationship with the earth. Often the protagonists are imprisoned in a subterranean labyrinth, symbol of the maternal womb. They yearn to rest again in earth's lap, as in "Palmuzza and the Bogeyman" and in "The Boy with the Little Golden Horns," in which Tamàr "every night in the deep darkness prayed to Adonài ... From there she gazed in silence at Mother Earth, who was shining, all in flower with climbing roses. She retraced her steps so far that she managed to find the long, long staircase ... She climbed back up, quite happy to find herself in her own land" (117).

In these tales, not only the earth, but all of nature takes on the aspect of the cosmic mother. In "Jesus and Giufà," the baby Jesus, bewildered, loses himself in the earth's womb; he adores the earth, while Giufà becomes its protector. Nature is present in both her aspects: violent and benign (sometimes even within the very same tale, as in "The Pumpkin") and in fact, in all of her cyclical mutations (birth and death, spring and winter, hot and cold, and so on), which are common to mother earth and to human life. And so the cosmic mother is at times presented as the locus of apocalyptic events. In the tale "St. Peter Plays the Violin, St. John Plays the Trumpet, and Jesus Destroys the World," the cosmic mother gathers into the abysm of her womb the planet earth, which is destroyed, while in "The Death of Jesus," out of that very same abyss the world is born.

One of the figures in the *Novelle Saracene* that gradually assumes maternal aspects is the village of Minèo, the umbilical cord of Bonaviri's universe, the mother who gathers all her children into her lap. Minèo is described as being seated on a mountain (84), as though on a throne. The maternal symbolism is made stronger by an association with St. Agrippina, patron saint of Minèo, who brings joy to the hearts of everyone. This is the theme of the tale "The Animals."

Another maternal image is the moon which, with its slow movement of rising and setting, of waxing and waning, has long suggested the condition of pregnancy, in addition to its being a figure of time and eternity. The moon presents its maternal aspects in "Jesus on the Moon," where it becomes the light that brightens the chthonic world. Another recurring symbol of maternity, carrying religious overtones, is milk, a symbolism which is developed throughout the entire tale entitled "Jesus Becomes a Mouse."

Yet another archetype, one that takes on maternal aspects (those of the "dio-femmina"), is the tree, which in mythology may give birth to human beings or to hero figures, or may close itself around other beings, whether as protection or as punishment. In these Saracen Tales, the tree is essentially a divine and maternal symbol of refuge: in "Jesus and Giufà," for example, the Saracen Jesus, pursued by the knights of King Frederick II, protects himself by hiding in a pine cone, and in "Jesus' Brother," the apostles take refuge in an olive tree.

Another image carrying religious and maternal associations is the reed basket, which often plays a role in saving the mythic hero at birth, either because he must be rejected, or as the result of a prophecy, or because the birth itself must be concealed. The baby may be handed over to a shepherd, who is ordered to kill the child, but who, out of kindheartedness, cannot bring himself to do so, and thus the basket is launched, like a tiny boat, onto a river or into the sea. The hero is thus saved by one who assumes a parental role, as happens in "Jesus' Brother" and in "The Twins as White as Lilies." The floating basket, no less than the waters that rock this cradle, takes on the maternal connotations of nurturing and bathing. In "Jesus Becomes a Mouse" the water-mother takes pity on the thirsty world-child: "it made the rain ... the grass sprouted on the languishing rocks" (81).

To sum up, the language of the *Novelle Saracene* brings a new vista to Bonaviri's stylistic panorama, enriching it with what Bonaviri himself has called a maternal language: "I have tried to recreate, in a joyful and exhilarating way, the language of women, the maternal language. The language of women creates something subtle, emotive, it carries with it centuries of experience ... mine is a metaphorical language, reinvented ... it is the blood of my blood ... After having written so many books, I have come at last to the core of this maternal language" (see Franco

Zangrilli, *La forza della parola. Incontri con Cassola, Prisco, Pomilio, Bonaviri, Saviane, Doni, Pontiggia, Altomonte* [Ravenna: Longo, 1992], pp. 91-93). This language has come about precisely because Bonaviri makes use of certain cadences, rhythms, and turns of phrase – narrative expedients, echoing the cadences, rhythms, the dialect phrases that were sealed in the author's memory from tales his mother had told him repeatedly in his infancy. Although it is difficult to compare Bonaviri's language to the linguistic experimentation of Verga or of certain neorealist writers, it is nonetheless accurate to state that Bonaviri's work is sustained by a language of "bewitching novelty" (see G. Spagnoletti, "Bonaviri: un mondo di burlesca sapienza," [*Il Tempo*, Rome, 29 March 1980], p. 3). His language, while echoing the cadences of the maternal narration, reveals also the author's distinctive predilection for adjectives used to convey sensations, for onomatopoeia, for humor, for an apparent simplicity and clarity in the expression of things and ideas – in all of which consists the beauty of this maternal, religious, collection of tales.

ESSENTIAL BIBLIOGRAPHY

Atti del convegno dedicato a G. Bonaviri. Tabella di Marcia. 4 maggio 1983.

Bertoni, Roberto, ed. *Minuetto con Bonaviri. Quaderni di cultura italiana* (Dublin: Trinity College, Italian Department), 2001.

Di Biase, Carmine. *Giuseppe Bonaviri. La dimensione dell'oltre*. Naples: Cassitto Editrice, 1994.

_____. *Bonaviri e l'oltre. L'opera intera*. Naples: Edizioni Scientifiche Italiane, 2001.

Di Biasio, Rodolfo. *Bonaviri*. Florence: La Nuova Italia, 1978.

Special Issue on Giuseppe Bonaviri. *La Fusca* VI, nos. 1-2, Spring-Fall 1981.

Iadanza, Antonio, and Marcello Carlino, eds. *L'opera di Giuseppe Bonaviri*. Rome: La Nuova Italia Scientifica, 1987.

Musarra, Franco. *Scrittura della memoria. Memoria della scrittura. L'opera narrativa di Giuseppe Bonaviri*. Florence: Franco Cesati Editore, 1999.

Zangrilli, Franco. *Bonaviri e il mistero cosmico*. Abano Terme: Piovan Editore, 1985.

_____. *Bonaviri e il tempo*. Catania: Marino Editore, 1986.

_____. *Il fior del ficodindia. Saggio su Bonaviri*. Catania: La Cantinella, 1997.

_____. *Sicilia isola-cosmica. Conversazione con G. Bonaviri*. Ravenna: Longo Editore, 1998.

Zappulla Muscarà, Sarah, ed. *Giuseppe Bonaviri*. Catania: Giuseppe Maimone Editore, 1991.

Zappulla Muscarà, Sarah, and Enzo Zappulla, eds. *Bonaviri inedito*. Catania: La Cantinella, 1998.

Author's Note

Giuseppe Bonaviri

With these tales I seem to have found a place of encounter with the most profound sentiments that I share with my people and with my mother. The narration of stories is the endless pursuit of Desire. In my homeland, the act of narrating stories was like a sheath that enveloped us (not unlike a placenta), and artisans and peasants came to a realization of their existence within this oral tradition. By this means we passed from the bleak reality of toil and poverty into a deeper sense of the real, where one might become a demon or a god, or even a supreme intellect, capable of calling anything and everything into being.

These little tales, dear mother, which you used to tell to me and my brother and my three sisters — Vincenza, Maria, & Ida —, you have now written down in two notebooks, in your cramped woman's hand, the writing of someone with only a rudimentary formal education. These tales carry with them a thousand desires, a thousand inventions that could transform a thought into a shining stone, into gold, into the song of birds. I have brought to these tales my own memories and humors as well, but their root in the Sicilian soil Is clearly revealed by the diffuse Mediterranean light that illumines them; by the balance between lighthearted ballads and dramatic *laude*; by the reverberations of myth. If one listens to them carefully, many of these fables, with their different delicate dramas and with their suggestion of balladry, the feminine voice can be heard so clearly that one might even speak of a matrilineal practice of narration. Two stories will suffice as examples.

In "The Lover Made of Honey," a young girl exists in a vacuum, that is, she lives her life within a closed system, from which she feels it is impossible to escape. But by giving rein to her profound sense of material reality, she manages to create for herself, with her own hands, a lover made of sugar and honey. That is, by pursuing an idea – or rather, a Platonic ideal –, and by infusing it with her feminine spirit – delicate, subtle, yet forceful –, she discovers herself in the creation of an imaginary other.

In the tale "The Twins as White as Lilies," we see the flourishing of the myth of the underground, from the depths of which grow the seeds of every earthly plant. In this tale, as a consequence of the dark deeds of his mother, a king (representing the organizing principle of earthly events) orders that his young wife be buried, but when the truth finally becomes known and she is freed, spring bursts forth on every side. What we have in the tale of Proserpina is a Sicilian version of the Greek myth of Persephone.

There is a patrilineal practice of narration as well, for example, in the tale of Pelosetta, which was one of two stories that I heard from my father (the other was "The Pumpkin"). My father told stories in his quiet, hesitant voice, marked by impassioned fits and starts. Pelosetta, a different version of the well-known Cinderella, becomes the incarnation of the rebellious Sicilians – here identified as Saracens – against French occupation.

Most of these tales form part of an ethnographic inheritance that may be considered Indo-European, if not truly universal, but they have clearly undergone notable changes, revealing a typically Sicilian cadence and style of recitation. This is especially so in the first section of this little volume ("Jesus and Giufà"), in which the stories – containing many layers, both ethnohistorical and magical – are presented as an epic of knightly chivalry, a narrative form so familiar to the Sicilian peasant. And so, my dear mother, we find the ingenuous Giufà side by side with Orlando, symbol of errant strength, and with Jesus, rendered as the indigenous figure of the wandering Saracen. It is as if our peasant, held fixed by a centuries'-old destiny between the town and the countryside, wished to create a Holy Trinity of heterodox personages, all of them prepared, in their eternal wanderings, to forge a story, whether by means of Orlando's sword Durendal, or by means of Giufà's comic ingenuousness, or by means of the play of miracles that flowered eternally in the mind of the peasant Jesus. What ensues, however, is that King Frederick II of Swabia, encouraged in his actions by the Pope, pursues this Saracen Jesus, subjecting him, along with Giufà and Orlando, to suffer a torture unto death, inflicted by his falcons. In this way, the usual story of the Christ, and the norms of christological thought, are transformed into a pagan, or at least, pre-Christian, drama, mirroring the encounter between two cultures, two powers, two opposing cultural myths. Everything is subject to a transformation, right down to the very place and time and way of understanding the Divine.

I also recall that often in October and November, the other peasant boys and I seemed to hear the blare of Orlando's horn, when the puppeteer Don Mariddu would come to town, together with the knights and the dark Saracens whom we would see emerging from the posters that illustrated their heroic deeds, and which were tacked up in the piazza.

And so, my sweet mother, in these tales, you and I meet again, just as we used to, in the High Street, or outside of town, near the city walls, where our house faced the little path, dug out of tufo and clay, amidst clumps of nettle and white artemisia, in the midst of which the hens laid their eggs.

These tales also contain a certain jocular wisdom, made more biting by the method of narration, by the inclusion of nonsense and the injection of rapid-fire dialogues. I also hear in these tales the sound of the *zufolo,* the little flute, that we as children — my brother, and Peppi Amarù, and I — used to play, standing on the rocky earth of Camùti, turning our eyes heavenward, toward the sleeping skylark as it held steady in the sky, in a fluttering of wings, or turning toward the earth, toward the sounding reed, toward the rocks, toward the ground, which yielded up the soft speech of dancing spirits.

But perhaps the greatest point of contact, dear mother, is to be found not so much in the images, but in the very language of these tales which, over centuries of stratification, has unlatched the frame that had fixed its syntax. This narrative language is a dialect that draws its life-giving spirit from every part of the visible world: from the song of the birds in the olive trees, from the movement of the stars sending forth cosmic rays and magnetic bands; from the tiny molecular vibrations of the grain and beans in their growth; from the falling of rocks; from the speech of the many peoples who passed through Sicily in successive, reviving waves. This is why, in the telling of stories, one form of verbal expression gives way to another, articulating, unconsciously, the different dimensions of time and space that define each character. Every phrase served as a kind of small retaining wall which, even though crumbling and gaping, separated the orchards from stretches of countryside, marking out riverbanks and clumps of reddish flowers. We tellers of tales live in a delirium of invention, in which reality is transfigured, as by a movie camera with which a director broadens or shortens the changing visual field What evolved was a play of syntax shot through with emotion. It was the search for the god who would give life to the imagination. In this way, language, essentially oral in nature, gives voice to new situations, complex emotions, subtle exclamations, soothing lullabies, which issue forth from poor peasant men and women, like operatic arias in the art of dramatization. This language is like a rainbow – at one extreme leading upward to the solar god, and at the other, leading downward to the god of the underworld. It is a language that expresses a fertile imagination, drawing from the sun on the one hand, and from the earth on the other. Or to use more rhetorical terms, we make use of a dialect that is realized in metaphoric ascents, rather than in metonymic leveling.

But what is essential is the place of encounter that you and I, dearest mother, have managed to discover after the extensive travels of our minds: the place where we meet in these stories is like a suture, or a biological concrescence, in which we two have always existed.

Nonetheless, as is the case with any book, and in a wider sense, as is the case with any human act, no matter our desires, another skin is shed, another spirit vanishes from deep within us, and what remains is the play of corporeal words with which we attempt to speak to one another, and to the goat, to the sparrow, to the fish, to the trembling leaf, to our lava rock.

Giuseppe Bonaviri

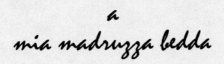

a
mia madruzza bedda

Jesus and Giufà

Jesus and Giufà

In her shop Maria sold jugs, pitchers, urns, jars, and pots large and small, which the cart drivers, crossing valleys, crags, and torrents, brought to foreign lands. In the winter Maria also sold dates, figs, roasted chestnuts, and small loaves of bread.

One day she became pregnant, she was expecting a child, and her soul was lost in the rays of the moon that reflected on the brambles and bushes. She left her shop and went to a mountain where she wished to give birth in seclusion, praising God. The father was perhaps Milùd, an Arab, son of Zacri, and Zacri, son of Malcom, and Malcom, son of Omar, and Omar of Muahlil, who was son of Mahmùd.

To serve as a lesson for us mortals, and in praise of our Lord called Macone, let us say that one stormy night, in a cave, Maria gave birth to a son.

"What should I name him?" she asked herself. Outside the night was raging.

She heard a voice: "Name him Jesus." She said: "Jesus? What kind of a name is that?"

This voice welled up from her very own heart: "O, foolish girl, don't you know that he will save the world, and before him, with his black hair, the grass, the star in the sky, the poor old woman will bow down."

"Let it be Jesus."

Maria, out of shame because she did not know who the father was, left the baby in the cave. She went away after three days, and the clarion call of the night sounded through the plains and valleys. As clear day was returning, with bright clouds on the mountain, a ewe passed by there, searching for her lamb, lost in the recent storm that had broken even the wing of an elf hidden in an olive tree.

The ewe hears a cry, she runs crashing through blackberry bushes, wormwood, and catnip. She finds the hidden cave, and on the straw she sees the little baby. He seemed to her to be one of her own lambs. She nursed him, like a plump, rosy mother, for two years, a month, and a day.

Let's leave the lamb who carried the baby into a little grotto near a flowing brook, and go back to Maria, who returns to the cave and doesn't find her little son. She cried, she said, "O Jesus, my ill-born child, falcon, dove, lily, where are you?"

She didn't find him. Full of sorrow, she returned to the village.

The sheep-mother continued to feed him with delicious fruits and berries. He grew big: now he was eight years old, and went running through the countryside. He gathered mistletoe, brambles, and palm fronds, and made himself a crown. The farmers who met him sometimes called him "Jesus," sometimes "Our Lamb." He learned the speech of men from the sighs of the barley, from the faint cry of the shadows, and from the thick speech of the peasants. And so he adored the Wind that gave him counsel as it blew over the rushing stream, the Honeyberry tree, the garrulous Blackbird, and the devout Sheep.

What sweet dreams the sight of our village awoke in him when he saw it there on the mountain under a bright burning sun! He went there with the ewe who was following him. As he was arriving, in heavenly light, the dawn was breaking.

On the way he meets a cobbler.

"Child, little child, where are you going?"

"To this village."

"With your black face, you look like a Saracen, like me. In this village – which in the past used to be ours – these days we are like the spider dangling by a thread over a ravine."

"What do you mean?"

"I mean that our King and Lord (may God Macone protect him), Ased-ibn-Forât-ibn Sinân, a Great Doctor, was conquered by King Frederick, our most ferocious enemy. Be careful, be careful."

Jesus didn't know anything about these matters. As we've said, he adored the Wind and the Sun.

"What's your name?" asked the cobbler.

"My name is Jesus."

"Jesus? Can this be? Then you are the child of my sister Maria. Oh how long she has been suffering and searching for you! I am Maria's brother. My name is Michael Gabriel. We Saracens live in great fear now." These two became friends: they were nephew and uncle. When the Saracen children saw the cobbler Michael arriving with Jesus, they sang with delight:

> Little child, dance and dance.
> The air belongs to you.
> Wherever you set your tiny foot,
> Basil and mint appear.

Don Michael didn't want to let his sister know right away. Her heart was shattered from the sorrow she felt because of her child, left abandoned in a cave in the mountains where the storm broke.

But you know how it is with people: *psst, psst, psst, buzz, buzz, buzz,* they let signora Maria know. She, in her joy, felt seven tongues in her mouth and a heart burning with love.

The meeting took place in the Santa Maria district, one day in midsummer. All the better that King Frederick wasn't there: he was amusing himself, watching his falcons in the wooded forest where they were flying with talon-like beaks. When he passed by, the Christians threw themselves respectfully at his feet. But let's leave Frederick who goes on his way alone through the woods and go back to signora Maria.

"My son?" she said to the Saracen woman who told her the news.

"Your son, Mother of sorrows."

"Run!" said another woman. "Why are you waiting here, like a ninny?"

The meeting took place. Jesus, poor eight-year old child, was full of fear and happiness. In truth, the only mother he knew was the ewe. Out of respect, he knelt down before this woman-mother. The women formed a circle around them, grasping each others' dark hands, and said:

> O sorrowful wound
> now become joyful!
> O divine love,
> O lovely and delightful love!
> O Jesus, our beautiful lamb.

That's how they talked. It is rough speech, as you know. His mother immediately gave her son something to eat: cheese from sheep's milk, salted ricotta, red pepper spread on the bread that is our sweet friend. There was a big party. Everyone was happy. O pure love and world that unites Mother and Child!

It got dark, it was evening. When day returned, his mother made this speech to her son:

"You are eight years old now. You can't keep wandering through the fields and gloomy riverbanks in the sun. You must take a master."

And what better master than Uncle Michael? He had a shop near the Salèmi Walls, where the village ends and slopes off, through stone piles and dry mayflowers, into a valley. He had a bench, shoetrees, hammers (one was made of silver, for the shoes of the gentlemen), leather, yellow and green twine. Jesus cried. He had no head for work – he was used to watching the skylark fly over the wheat, and to sucking milk from his sheep-mother.

But he quickly learned the trade. At first he hammered the soles which had been set in water to soften. Then he learned to drive the awl into the right place. And his uncle:

"Jesus, do this. Jesus, do that."

Giufà, the son of Magdalene, also went to work in that shop. Everyone knows he was born with a weak brain. He didn't understand too well. He thought only of eating bread spread with olive oil and pepper. He was all shoulders, he was very sturdy. At first, he got up to mischief, chasing hens or the rooster, filling up his fists with ants, catching the little white cloud that in the evening followed the purple moon.

"Oh, what a nice mess! You here with me, too?" said Don Michael the cobbler when he saw him. "May the will of our God Macone be done."

Giufà – who was born, they say, on the same day as Jesus – wasn't much for work. In fact, if he saw the dust whirl around the crying nettles, he said, "Oh, sad wind, are you making my friends the nettles cry?" He went out to protect them with his body. He painted them blue. He made polish for Master Michael from the drops of the nettle plant.

Compared to Giufà, Jesus was little, with a dark face, and never still, like a spinning top. He liked to see the Sparrow, the Partridge, the Swallow fly in their beautiful dark garb. When the cicadas were heard to sing, along with the peasants who were threshing grain trodden by mules turning on the threshing floors, Michael Gabriel, in that indolent noonday sun, taught those boys other things: he explained how Time was born, how Man dies and then goes walking in the asphodel meadow. He taught them about the movements of the worlds scattered in the sky. Giufà said: "Are you making all this up?" Jesus, more careful, with a polite pretense of belief, said, "Uncle and dear friend, you know so many things: why can't you make me fly like the birds?" And Uncle Michael, dear friend, cobbler:

"Ha, ha, ha."

One day by those desolate Salèmi Walls, an old woman was killing a bold rooster.

"Will you give me the wings?" asks Jesus.

Signora Marasanta, the rooster-killer, replied, "Take them, you sure won't make any soup out of them."

"With these wings I am going to learn to fly."

"Ha, ha, ha."

Jesus thinks it over. He spoke to Giufà and to Uncle Michael. Giufà laughed: "Great idea, great." His uncle stared at him wide-eyed, but he saw Jesus' eyes burning with tears.

"OK," he said.

Don Michael Gabriel's mind wasn't dull, but fresh as laurel in the wind, so what did he do? With twine, ropes, cotton, and interlacing knots, he attaches the wings to Jesus. Jesus was very happy. Meanwhile his uncle was telling him that meekness, patience, and chastity are good things. Even Giufà gladly helped attach the quivering wings with the feathers of a thousand eyes.

"Do it, Jesus," he said, "Fly, fly."

He tries, tries again, hops and jumps. Under his feet the rock grows lighter. He flew along the doorways, very low. His eyes took in everything. An old woman: "Oh, what are you doing, you little devil? You're flying? Just now when the sun is leaving and the sigh of the night is coming on?"

A little girl, with a shout of terror, "Hey, Jesus is flying."

So, this child learns to fly: now sideways, now with his hands open like shining feathers, now using his chest. A peasant, seeing him, said to him: "O Jesus, you animal, if you fall you'll break your neck." His uncle, dear friend and kin, was so happy. With a proud voice and a shining face he said to the people: "Do you know that my nephew can fly?"

Now Jesus managed to go above the roofs, where he felt the burning hot sound of the sun that penetrated the climbing herbs.

One time Orlando and Rinaldo, still young, with graceful faces and gentle speech, happened to be passing through. They were wandering through the world because of the hatred of King Frederick, who had killed Charlemagne and his divine virtue. According to Theopompus, they had to wander for 233 years. So... They stopped at Uncle Michael Gabriel's house to have him fix the nails on their leg guards and the small cords of their shields.

"At your service, knights," said Don Michael. But seeing them weary and discouraged, he said, "Be calm, O Orlando, Rinaldo, cousins of noble lineage, because to our God Macone belong the East and the West, and wherever you turn to pray, there is the face of our God. For from him will be born smaller and wiser gods."

And that's how these two cousins happened to see Jesus who, in low flight, his eyebrows knit, was flapping his wings.

"Oh, this is great," they said. "Are you perhaps the son of Astolfo who flies on the horse Pegasus? Or the son of a cloud that opens up in a storm?"

Then they discovered who he was. They laughed and made friends. These knights were boys too. Rinaldo set his bejeweled cloak on the ground, he wanted to try to fly. Jesus said to him, "Do this, do that!" He couldn't do it. The cousins laughed, and bidding farewell to the peasants who were there, to Master Michael, and to Jesus and Giufà, they set out again through the world of adventure. Their iron footsteps, joined to the clanging of their swords, could be heard as the moon, reclining in its shell, rising from the abyss, showed its face over the streets of the village.

Jesus, under the light of the oil lamp, took up his work, hammering soles. The moon was shining in its shell. Orlando and Rinaldo were headed towards the shining Ardennes.

But one day, what happens? King Frederick, returning to his castle where he used to amuse himself, along with his notary and with the ladies playing mandolas, was told:

"Your Majesty the King, there is a Saracen who flies."

"What are you saying, my man? Have you lost your mind?"

"He flies, Sacred Majesty and Honored One."

"A Saracen?"

"Yessir."

"Are there still Saracens in my kingdom?"

Once, awakened from a deceptive noonday sleep, and leaning out of the castle tower, he did in fact see that little wretch fly. He watched him through his telescope. He saw his graceful movements, his bright shining wings. At first he thought of taking him on as his little squire, but then: "A Saracen? Never!" His eyes blazed. He sent up one of his noble falcons to capture the little child. The bird hesitated at first, shook his head, then shot upwards, spiraling in the air. But the Saracen Jesus escaped, folded his wings, and dropped to earth like a bird.

The King shouted: "Warriors! Summon my warriors!"

At that loud cry that was like a chant, the notary came. There were 1000 knights, like lions and bears.

"Your Majesty, here we are. What is your command?"

The King gave orders to search for Jesus. The Christian people were happy. "That little Saracen must die. He wants to rise higher than our King."

Swiftly and deftly a woman ran, and she said to Uncle Michael the cobbler, "By the holy olive tree, by our God Macone, save the little child."

And so this is what happened. The good folk, quickly moved to tears, said, "O God, save him! O Allah, our God!" Jesus, who was resting in the midst of the white artemisia herb, saw a goatherder who said to him: "Run away, my boy, the Christian knights of the King are coming to arrest you." The rascal Jesus went off, through the rocks of Ballarò, where there are only pines with branches that, in beautiful shapes, open to the sun. They were female pines of the kind that drop fruit and sing to the zephyr wind if it catches them. Now Jesus, what does he do? He hides himself in a pine cone. He manages to do it by dint of effort and palpitation. That pine cone was lamp, bed, and cave to him. This is true: in fact, if you open a pine cone, inside you will find small pods that look like little hands joined together, all sweet and white. They are the hands of Jesus.

But the poor child could not live forever in the tree. He loved the shining star, the poor people, and out of his compassion, he had to save the world.

Meanwhile King Frederick is getting angry. "How can it be that he cannot be found?" he asked the soldiers, who had searched for him for a year, a month, and a day, in hopes of finding him. The Pope was told of the matter in the Spring, as he was languishing, watching our planet flower in the blue sky.

"A Saracen?" he said.

"Yes, Your Holiness," the King informed him.

"Search for him throughout the lands and the deep seas. So be it. Amen."

And the Pope also sent his soldiers, armed to the teeth. Through paths and blood-red clumps of earth they went. But Jesus had come out of the pine cone and had mixed in among the other boys of Minèo. How could anyone recognize him? His uncle the cobbler had said to him: "Jesus, don't come near me anymore. You will be found out. Go find work."

The olives were ripe; they were falling in the valleys and knolls. Our countryside was in bloom with them. The birds flew in the midst of them. They pecked at the olives with their beaks. The buyers who came from Militello sent the boys to buy the olives – boys work for less, they eat only bread, and they get used to the freezing rays of the evening.

Giufà went to work with Jesus. He didn't leave him, for he had become fond of him. There were two other boys, Turi and Peppi. They went from neighborhood to neighborhood where the day was dying.

The boys: "O, ladies, who has olives to sell? O, ladies!"

They filled the sack that they carried on their backs. Their song was lost in the streets. Sleep came to their graceful eyes. The bell sweetly tolled the two hours of night; it was time to sleep.

"O, ladies, who has olives to sell?"

"Who has olives?" repeated Giufà in a hoarse voice that grew weaker.

Some old women, seeing those children, out of the kindness of their hearts, gave them bread.

"The big slice is bread. Make believe the little slice is cheese," they said.

Around midnight, darkness issued forth even from the stones. In drips and drops it fell from the roofs. At these times in November, the rain comes to our land and to the dark mountains – not the hard rain that washes and scents the air, but a very fine rain, which is welcome news for the fields that await it with open mouths. Our poor little children got drenched. They felt a hollow softness in their little bones, and they sat down on the ground, resting their heads on stones or on their sacks. There was a strong fragrance. It was the smell of olives that spreads all around like the feathers of the moon. They fell asleep. There was no more peal of the bell. Jesus and Giufà and Turi and Peppi saw in their dreams the white-footed nymph, or perhaps God, who, yawning, issued forth from the mouth of a donkey.

And so the little child took sick, and his mother, spied on by the Normans, could not help him. The imperial arm of the King was felt throughout the land. Magdalene, mother of Giufà, took Jesus in, for she had a house outside the village, near the Walls. From there, in that month, you could see the horrible clouds that rise up steaming, covering the valleys and the sky. Jesus contracted malaria, which comes to us from the plain in breaths of wind, carried by the cold and by winged insects in flight.

"Is he another child of yours?" asked some kind-hearted women. "What's the matter with him?"

"He has malaria," said Magdalene, who explained that he wasn't a son, but a nephew by blood. She did this, you understand, to prevent his being captured by the treacherous soldiers who wandered through the village and mountains in vain pursuit. Magdalene, sorrowing, put a little cloak over Jesus, and he sat before the door, looking out over the deserted walls where evening was dissolving like mist. The old men – Farmer Giuseppe or Farmer Angelo Mangiapicca – breathed as hard as they could to warm the Little Child. For he was shivering with cold because of the malaria, which is a huge wandering light of frozen shadows. Magdalene, to give him courage, said to him: "O my little Jesus, beautiful lily, many children in the village shiver with cold. It's a sickness, like bad air. Even the frog, the wolf, the red rabbit, and the clump of earth in the field catch it."

In fact, even the birds in the olive trees were shivering from the malaria that brought with it kingdoms of the dead. Besides, November was a rainy month.

So.

Let's leave Jesus and go back to Orlando and Rinaldo, who

learned of the matter.

"You two are here?" said a Saracen, whom Uncle Michael the cobbler had sent on purpose to look for them.

"And where should we be?" said Orlando.

"Jesus has malaria, he's shivering. Oh, infernal gates of fever."

They ran. Orlando said to Rinaldo, who was tarrying to take a last look at the gardens full of oranges and at the star Ursa Major: "O, are you getting lost in visions? Run, Jesus is sick."

They went again through the twisted slope, where capers grew. The rocks shed some flakes because of the wind.

"O Orlando, O Rinaldo," the old people cried out in recognition. "Save us from the evil malaria."

But what could they do? Could they, with their swords Durendal and Fusbert, combat that evil that sprang up and afflicted the world? Do you know what they thought up? From the walls, with their beautiful shields, edged with cords of gold, they directed the dazzle of the setting sun upon those freezing old people, and upon the little child Jesus. The doors turned white. The crown on Jesus' head was illumined. Virtue shone amidst the green fronds. And so everyone was happy, very happy. The people began to say:

"What, has the sun risen again?"

But Orlando and Rinaldo had things to do. Ferrau and Sacripante had to run through the shimmering gardens, with pendulous oranges and tangerines. So they set off again.

"Jesus, we'll meet again," said Orlando. "Fight off that sickness."

Giufà didn't leave Jesus, he shared even his sleep that came raging with fever. One day, when the little child was feeling better (though his face was as yellow as a branch in October), Giufà, to amuse him, said to a nail:

"Nail, little nail, turn into fine gold."

"What are you saying, you idiot, my child and ruination? Don't you know you'll upset poor little Jesus this way?" his mother said to him.

But the nail sparkled. O divine power of Giufà!

"Ah," his mother Magdalene said, getting angry, "and does this seem like the right time to be performing miracles?"

Giufà, however, felt himself on fire with love of the world. He said to a hundred flies who had settled on a beam of wood on the roof to warm themselves in that severe winter: "Turn into butterflies." And butterflies they were, they flew as though amidst roses, violas, and shadowy leaves.

"And still you want to play?" said Mother Magdalene. "Oh, you idiot of a child. Why didn't I break your head, just like I did to your other brainless brothers?"

The dust of the Walls was picked up by the wind. The nettles sang their lament. All the rocks felt trapped as though bound on a sad voyage.

Jesus was happy to see Giufà do so many strange things. A bat flew lightly by, and Giufà said: "Turn into a sparrow." And a sparrow it became, that trilled on its reed pipe.

To entertain the little Child, he also invented different instruments, like a little whistle, a pipe with seven holes, and a violin made of strings, leather, and olive bark. He used them to attract animals. Cautiously the Blackbird, the Partridge, the blue-black Raven came forth.

Jesus, who was feeling better (the fever was no longer burning, it had died down), also wanted to play on the instruments to perform miracles. He played, but nothing happened. He didn't have Giufà's powers. For example, he said to the sparrow: "Turn into a blackbird." But the sparrow, to the honor of God Macone, remained a sparrow. He said to a stone: "Turn into bread." The stone raised itself up with an aching heart, but it did not turn into bread.

Mother Magdalene became furious: "Little Jesus, you, too! Leave life the way it is, dark and still! I've brought an inferno into my house!"

What's more, the good news had spread: *psst, psst, psst, buzz, buzz, buzz.* The poor people in the village learned of it. One woman: "Giufà, I have one loaf of bread. It's not enough. Will you change it into two loaves?" And Giufà, zap! and it was done.

Another woman, leading a shabby old goat with twisted horns: "Giufà, don't you see? It has no milk. Make its teats swell." And its teats swelled. The poorest ones came:

> There was Turi the artichoke,
> Cicciu the dogpisser,
> Ianu the matchstick,
> Puddu the hunchback,
> Peppi the doorpost,
> Matteu the olive vendor,
> Antoniu the asparagus-sucker,
> and Angiuzzu the chicory vendor.

They sang: "Little Jesus, when we unfortunates were born, / Our fate was bad luck. / For three days the sun remained hidden / and for four days the moon did not come out./ Whoever is born unlucky / dies that way;/ Whoever isn't lucky / can never be so."

There was such a coming and going that Magdalene's house could not hold so many people. Magdalene's face turned from black to red: "A sudden death to all of you! We are poor, and poor we remain. You can't get blood out of a stone. I can give you some dry bread and onions."

There was a chiming, a bell rang out. It was the bell of Santa Maria, and over the silent thresholds fell the gentle rain. Magdalene also handed out olives roasted over coals, and water that grew pale in the rushing streams. Jesus rejoiced to see all those people. He played his violin made of olive wood. Others played tambourines and pipes. The delight of the body was in harmony with the sounds. Amidst murmurings and the boom of distant thunder came the cold.

"Oh, how cold it is," said Ciccio Pòspero.

"Oh, how cold it is," said Farmer Angelo.

"You can complain all you want about the cold," wailed Magdalene, "but it doesn't help us a bit." And then, "Giufà, scourge of my life, a bad end to you and to your miracles! And now you're a bad influence on Jesus, too. Go to the woods immediately, and gather some wood. Right away, you son of Cain."

He went out. It had been three thousand, three hundred years since God had created the world, and the cold was always there. It burst out of the olive trees and the rocks. Giufà ran into the woods where the birds were white with ice. They didn't breathe, they couldn't open their beaks.

"You're frozen, too?" he said.

With a hatchet he cut down thorns and brambles. He filled his sack, and he set out again through the white paths, through the valleys without violets or lilies. People meeting him asked, "What are you carrying, Giufà?"

"Touch it, touch it and you'll see."

"Ouch! You're carrying thorns? Ouch!"

And he said, "It's easy to say something, it's another to do it." Arriving home, he calls to his mother: "Mother Magdalene, I'm bringing you wood."

She goes to touch it: "Ouch, are those thorns? O idiot child, o son without a brain! Run, hurry back to the countryside!"

That poor boy goes out again. He encounters the hornèd herd, the rushing stream in a black mantle. He sees an olive tree, all turned to ice. "I'll take this," he said to himself. And he took it. He put his brawny arms around it and he uprooted it. The olive tree shouted to the wind. It was entangled in the mists in the sky. Giufà arrived at his village.

"Mother Magdalene, come down. Help me."

"You've uprooted an olive tree! O sweet Jesus! O God Macone!" They chopped it up. There was enough for everybody. They built a fire. It sparkled through the branches. Even the sparrow warmed himself, and the donkey Rondello warmed his hooves.

But enough... all this came to an end. One day his mother had to go to the mosque.

"Giufà," she said, "now that the blood in our veins is turning to ice again, I am going to pray to the King God Macone, in the mosque. If the sun comes out, have it come into the house. And make some bread soup for your little brother who's in the cradle. Mind, now."

By now Jesus had gotten over his fever. He had no words for prayers. He wanted to hear the grain growing in the fields again. It's a delicate sound, recognized by those imbued with understanding.

Into the house of Magdalene came the sun. It was crying softly because it had pierced a cloud that had turned blue. And that idiot child, Giufà:

> Enter, enter holy Sun,
> mounting the porch.
> All the air is already cleansed,
> all the women are at the windows.

So, what does he do? He climbs up the stairs, and with his broad shoulders he breaks open the roof. The tiles and the supporting beams fell. There was a sea of sunshine. Then Giufà remembered his little brother who was six months old. He took four loaves of bread, crumbled them up, and boiled them in a pot. There was enough to feed four grown men. The sun had eyes of silver, and Giufà fed his little brother. He fed him and fed him until he got tired. His brother had bread coming out of his nose. His mother returned, she called out: "Giufà, have you done everything?"

"Everything, Mother Magdalene."

She enters. She's terrified: she sees sun everywhere, it was like quicksilver. She goes to look at her little son, and sees him with his mouth stuffed with bread and suffocating death.

"You have destroyed my house, you thieving child. You have destroyed my house. Hurry, women! Hurry, women!"

The judge came. He wanted to know everything. The sheriff was on the back of a pawing horse. Giufà ran through the village. He looked for Jesus ("Only he can help me," he thought), and he went to the shop of Uncle Michael Gabriel, who was bent over, making shoes.

"Uncle Michael cobbler, help me. The law is after me."

"The law is after you? Has King Frederick given the order? You're lost! And Jesus?"

"Help me, uncle and kin."

Uncle Michael Gabriel, like everyone in the village, which lacked water ("Minèo, rich in wine, poor in water," they used to say), had a cistern in his shop, and when the rain came in a tumultuous roar, it collected there, as though in a well. The water also relieved thirst.

"You know what I say, Giufà? Lower yourself into the cistern."

There was a rope. He lowered himself into the bucket. He wasn't a child to be afraid, not the way Jesus was. You could hear the sound of chains. Down there another world began. There was no cicada, but smoke and shadows and endless caves.

No one ever found Giufà. Later, Uncle Michael Gabriel the cobbler called to him, leaning down at the mouth of the cistern.

"O Giufà, my dear Giufà."

Maybe he answered him from far away, or maybe he couldn't hear him in that darkness without end. Later on, Magdalene wanted him, for her heart was always the heart of a mother. But she couldn't find him, and, crying, she said to the village woman who had asked about him: "You know what they say? Whoever has children, has ankles; whoever has gold, has gold and silver; whoever has silver and a son like Giufà, remains a fool."

The Resurrection of Giufà

*O*nce upon a time, it is told, Giufà slept for 300 years in a secluded valley whose depths were full of shimmering sapphires. Up on the hill that peacefully surrounded the valley grew fig trees, apricot trees, and almond trees. Spring would arrive there with hawks, hedgehogs, and small pensive horses. Giufà, as we know, had been lowered into a well when he was a boy, his black hair full of little stones of cryptolite, fermium, melancholy tellurium, iridium, polonium, sorrowing niobium, and dazzling molybdenum. These tiny little stones that collected in the abyss, falling on Giufà's head, little by little after so many years formed the moon that walks beneath our village in sweet lament.

So... Giufà, after this long sleep, woke up. He raised himself up like a hillock, and even the goddesses of the nether world, mixed with lanthanum and little particles of samarium, turned, lamenting, under the earth among the white chalk and the red cinnabar. Mother Magdalene, when she saw him, stunned and with his eyes reddened from sleep, said:

Would that I had never been born into the world!
At every approaching year
I sigh and frown.

The Christian women said in fear: "Alleluia, Alleluia!" Giufà, was the same big, black, fearless, unvanquished brute as ever. Everyone watched him come up from out of the earth.

Let's leave him and go to King Frederick, who, from his castle, was gazing through his telescope upon his endless land and the infinite sun. He saw everything: mountains, sea, robbers' hideouts, gardens, and the golden bay. As usual, his notary was entertaining him – and with him, the grass, the insect, the fleeing day – singing:

I've set my heart on serving God
and on going to a beautiful paradise where
I will save my soul in smiles and laughter.

"What is this resounding din?" Giufà asked himself, having come to the village. "In my day it didn't exist."

In fact, the sound of the lute hung in the air, the mandolin made waves of whiteness.

He was still shaking briars and clods of earth off his body, breaking up small clumps, scraping off mold and unsprouted buds of grain. The Christian people ran towards the castle with its thousand steaming windows.

"Your Majesty, Your Majesty, Our King and Lord, don't you hear us?"

"Oh, what do you want?"

"Giufà has risen from Mt. Carratabbìa. He's a ferocious Saracen. Save us!"

"Ha, ha!" laughed the King, and with him his soldier knights, armed with shields and swords. Laughing, the notary said, "Frederick, with his beautiful rosy face and his beautiful blond hair, cares not a whit for Giufà, with his black heart."

"Ha, ha," laughed the Christians, taking heart.

Giufà, in the meantime, also terribly angry over his interrupted sleep ("Oh, come on," his mother said to him), uprooted an olive tree, the one his father had planted.

"Let *Recàne* see it," shouted his mother.

Recàne, as you know, was Frederick, who had destroyed the Saracens and the wandering rose of the Sun. Indeed, the people, seeing this infuriated giant, escaped through the alleys and sad little streets. In the meantime, he arrives at the castle. The towers and windows were still shining, but the walls were bristling, twisted like sausages, and Giufà was still the Giufà he'd always been. He stays there for a day and a night.

"Hey, stupid," said his peasant friends, "Blow the ramparts to the sky. We'll help you." And they sang:

> *When this one dies, the wolf dies,*
> *When the wolf dies, the world grows;*
> *When the world grows, the bird flies,*
> *And the King lies in his grave.*

The knights defended themselves with arrows and bombards of lava stone that thundered in the dark air. The day was torment and fire.

"Ah," said the Saracen peasants, "You can fill the land with arrows, but we'll be waiting here."

The King closed himself up with his barons in the castle, where the day was blazing. They were playing guitars and mandolins. The sound flew away, fleeing like a bird. Frederick was singing:

> *But we, with great pleasure*
> *Kissing ladies with faces of silver,*
> *Adorn ourselves with laughter and art.*

And the Saracens below sang in chorus:

> *Beauty, like a rose, is a passing thing;*
> *They grow older, the bride and her King.*

Giufà was eating bread with pepper, and laughing, "Ha, ha." They couldn't stay holed up in their castle forever. One day, as it pleased God Macone, the bombardment and the arrows stopped. There was silence, and in the valley the cry of the nightingale was heard.

"The castle is ours!" the villagers shouted. "Hurray, Praise Allah!"

Giufà had blood in his eyes from the strength that was returning to him after resting so long and eating bread and pepper. He tore away some rocks, the holes in the walls got wider. The peasants, entering through those holes, found themselves facing knights with swords and helmets. The earth felt like lead. The soldiers' swords wheeled like woods in the fury of the wind, and many villagers would have died, but Giufà thrashed out to the left and to the right, and unbraided those twisted walls. Mother Magdalene, with her women friends, and Maria herself, the mother of Jesus, cried out from below on the plain, where midday was dimly shining:

> O child of my womb,
> Wonder of a new people,
> King of Sicily and Castile,
> Kill Frederick, kill him at once!

It is not known for sure if *Recàne* was wounded, but he freed himself from the hands of Giufà through the machinations of his notary who had made him a flying machine. He flew over the mountains of Arcura, he with his mantle all of red flowers, with his notary beside him who, clasping a Norman woman, sang:

> Without my lady I would not wish to leave,
> She with the blond hair and bright face
> Like the gentle, gentle wave of the sea.

After this event, Giufà had more tender feelings. He held the poor in respect. He protected his mother. He hated liars, and searched out the pure water of the streams. He set himself to being a cobbler, in memory of his dear friend, Uncle Michael Gabriel. He had a bench, a red cloak, yellow leather, black nails, and a songbird in a cage. Sometimes his mind would wander, and then he would go into the country where the sun beats down and causes the stones to die, and he would fill his pack with ants or with butterfly wings.

"Oh, what are you doing, Giufà?" asked the villagers, bent over the grain.

"Can't you see? Have you lost your head?"

"Are you gathering ants? Ha, ha."

"O you foolish villager, don't you know they are Allah's creatures? It is He who made the ant and the cicada, He who planted palm trees, who nourishes us with pomegranates and olives, He who tells us that alms should be given to the poor."

"You're not so dumb," remarked a villager, bent over the grain waving in the gusts of air.

And so the news got around.

"Did you know that Giufà knows the law of the Prophet?"

"Is that true?"

"Could it be?"

One old lady got the idea of making him king.

"Seeing as we don't have a king, why don't we make Giufà king?"

"Giufà?"

"The very same."

"He's pure of heart."

And so the women went to tell him while he was sleeping under a carob tree, waiting for the carob pods to fall from the tree around him so he could eat them.

"Wake up, Giufà!"

"Who's looking for me? Why don't you leave me in the breeze and shade at this hot hour?"

"Do you want to be our king?"

"Your king?"

And he laughed modestly and with a gentle laugh.

"Our king, yes."

"Ha, ha, ha."

And what with one thing and another, hearing about it day after day, he had it up to his ears with this idea of becoming king. And the villagers: "So what are you waiting for to become king, you beast?" He really and truly was like a big, dumb beast. Their request fell on deaf ears. But do you know what happened? In that propitious month of June, there appeared a marvelous comet with a very long tail that streaked through the sky like albumen. Some thought it was a star sent on purpose by the God Macone, others that it was an angel who brandished an incredibly bright scimitar. According to what St. Francis of Paola wrote, it exceeded in brightness all the other bodies. It was a dewy bed of the vault of heaven.

So Giufà took fright. He didn't think that the star was simply an object making its way through its stellar destiny, but was an order of the Prophet directed at him. And he said:

"So be it, so be it. I will be king."

The first thing he did was to call the town not Minèo, as the ancients had done, but Minàw, as Jesus Himself had intended, and his deceased father whom he had never known. The second thing he did was to bring from the nearby villages musicians, guitar players, tellers of stories and fables. Finally, he set up a search for Jesus, who was going through plains and valleys and along the river that goes murmuring by.

It is said that all this was found carved into a large shield found under the stones of our castle, which was destroyed by excessive solar heat and by the years. It was a very large shield with circular designs, and every circle told this plaintive story with figures. Anyway...

Meeting up with him, Jesus was very happy. By now he had wrinkled cheeks, but he continued to wander through the world with his companions, the apostles St. Peter, St. Joachim, St. Francis, and the youngest one, St. Francis of Paola.

"Master," said Giufà, "before becoming king I want to go about with you and learn again how to perform miracles."

This meeting – and you could see the tears stamped in silver under the darkened eyes of Giufà – was carved in threads and fine traces of gold in the second circle of the shield. And looking at it this way, the people could see what happened next.

To make it short and not bore the audience, Giufà, before becoming a bold king, became an apostle. They went through deserted lands where dried up rivers sink among rocks and powerful veined lava. He, the fool, wanted to learn. He gave heed to every word or to every noise which, like an lance, struck the air.

"Master, tell me, what is compassion? How does the flower become gentle on its stalk? What is this thing that poor people call 'love'?"

The Master smiled, his hair seemed blacker, his calamite-eye suddenly burned. In this way, ladies and gentlemen, Giufà re-learned some things. Naturally after 300 years of deep, lifeless sleep, his memory was frayed. If he touched an apricot, it ripened. If he touched a hen, it laid an egg. If he touched an almond tree, where a turtle-dove was fanning itself with its wings, the fruit ripened. Little things, but they were enough to make him happy, as you see in one circle where he, Giufà, is surrounded by the pullet, by the kindly moon rising over the valley, and by the soft beam. But the apostles were envious – they were men, after all. They made fun of Giufà if some miracle went up in smoke. They took the joyous light from his spirit. So he challenged them to fight. He turned his back on everyone – oh sad, evil, poisonous ones, what did you think, that Giufà couldn't handle this?

Jesus said to him, "Now you are ready to be king: you are strong, you know how to work miracles, you have understanding in your heart. Go!"

And so Giufà returned to Mlnàw. The guitar players and all the rest were waiting for him. In the village they played, they danced; the trumpet sounded in good company.

"What, is this all we're going to do, play? How are we going to eat?" asked the peasants, who were accustomed to meditate on a grain of wheat and on the spring fava bean. What did Giufà do? He called forth the birds. And his mother: "What do you think you're doing, my son, King of Castile and Sicily?"

"Quiet, you!"

Multitudes of birds arrived: sparrows, thrushes, crows, blackbirds, nightingales, and King Giufà gave those animals bits and crumbs of bread.

"O you beast," said the villagers. "You take away from us what little we have to give it to flying beasts?"

"Bring grain and beans!" ordered Giufà, King of Castile and

Sicily.

"Never, never."

The birds were many, they even came from over the sea in a blue flight of black claws.

The grain was brought with sad and bitter lament: it was the order of the King!

"Cast it down, o birds," he said, "throughout the valleys and quarries. Your soul thinks like ours." And do you know what happened?

> *No one was hungry anymore.*
> *Everyone, single or married,*
> *lived in a dream.*
> *Everyone had hopes,*
> *hunger went away.*
> *Everyone was beautiful*
> *and didn't get old.*

The rocks received rainwater, and inside them grain sprouted, oh so much grain. The happiness of our village was such that eyes cried and hair curled. Some sneezed, some coughed. Everyone's tongue was swollen with joy. This is exactly what can be seen in the shield of Giufà we mentioned. You can see in full flowering (worked in silver) fig trees, apple trees, almond trees, and reddish prickly pears. There was a plenitude of branches and of light, and the sun grew soft over the groves of olive trees. They say that Giufà made trees grow there that had never been seen before – they were called orange trees, with red leaves and boughs.

He, Giufà, was good at being King and the Lord Our Savior. The land smelled of dust and mint. The most devout women, those without lies in their hearts, sang and recited a new song:

> *Signor Giufà, you have risen;*
> *grass, olive trees, and crickets*
> *have taken up song again,*

in life without death.

The rich people asked him, "*Signore*, will you give me another large fief?" And he, ready to give it to them, painted a fief and fronds on the tired laborers, on the stony places, on the cicadas.

The not-so-rich asked him, "Will you give us mules, horses, barns?" And he was ready to fashion in clay young mares and a benefice of dewy grain. The poor said, "Will you give us bread and wine?" And Giufà sculpted bread in the rocks, and wine in the water.

But, seeing the rich get richer, the women with poisonous tongues asked themselves, "Is this any way to administer justice? Where will we all end up?"

Giufà, whenever he got hungry, began to act up. Then he would say, "*Corpus meum, corpus meum!*" and this meant that it was time to eat, and to cast off melancholy affliction. The apostles and the soldiers ran to him right away. Without a murmur they brought him salted ricotta, bread spread with oil and pepper, and sweets made with honey. He picked at them, and then he had no pity on anyone. Piteously the women would bring him baskets of prickly pears, of almonds already shelled. Once he had satisfied his hunger and his mind, Giufà felt good only if he slept under his carob tree, hidden in its shadows. Afterwards Giufà would give health to the sick, bread and beautiful fronds to the children. And the women, as was their custom, would say:

> *O dark and joyful son of ours*
> *King Most High of Castile and Sicily,*
> *Our light and consolation*
> *Praise be to you and to the moon and stars.*

He had given the order to cast out of the temples and churches the statues of the saints (St. Peter took offense, his heart darkened), the portraits of the beautiful Madonnas, not genuine, the sacred cloths that adorned the columns and the altars.

"Out with it, out with it! O, my people, Our God says: 'Do not overstep the bounds, nor follow the desire of people who in the past were led astray by false gods, straying from the straight way'. God is invisible, and he is not alone because he has behind him many other gods."

Thus spoke that big brute. But in matters of religion, not everyone obeyed him. There were many Christians who, in secret, built a temple in a hidden valley where they carved on the walls the same God in many forms, now sorrowing, now happy, now in meditation, now terrible, with one hand pointing to Hell.

When Giufà, poor child, learned of it, he became angry, but naturally he could not have so many Christians killed. He thought of the tranquil dawn, his carob tree where the nightingale sang, the clouds that glow so softly over Mt. Carratabbìa, and he no longer wished to be King.

"And who says I have to? What am I, crazy?"

His mother said, "My dear little Giufà, hold on, this will pass. What better fate than King?"

"Never, never. Enough!"

He went away when evening came, pale as the olive. No one ever heard anything more of him. We believe that in the story of antiquity one can find no voices more sorrowful than those of the men and women who called to him from oak trees, from almond trees, from the roof where our Lady the moon walks.

"O Giufà, our King and wealth! O Giufà!"

There was no longer any joy. The baptized were unbaptized. No longer did the grain wave on the plains and in the valleys. The rich became poor, and the poor even poorer.

In the sky the stars are shining. The story ends here, with no ending!

Jesus on the Moon

In our realm, there were no longer joyous thick woods in mirth, and so Jesus returned. The people had said to him:

"Master, what are you waiting for? Your village is becoming depopulated. The snail is dying, the blackbird flies no more, the moon does not rise up out of the depths."

The countryside was no longer green and fresh. The hornet wandered there without finding any lizards. Jesus arrived. He was still in his youthful beauty, and to give joy, he was followed all around by very beautiful girls, with garlands of myrtle and laurel. Sometimes these girls, incited by the spurs of love, undressed, and Jesus forgot his splendid chastity, his hands pricked him like darts. In the village one could hear:

"What's going on?"

"The world is changing."

"It's not like it used to be, that's for sure."

The Angel Gabriel Michael reproached the naked young girls in the glory of love like the dawn. Even the scarce dry grass became anxious, and twisted this way and that. In our realm the sun was always there, blazing down on everything.

To make the earth green again, Jesus, the holy apostles, and the women planted grapevines that grew joyously. They called them *àmpelos*.

Truly, they flourished in great splendor, and the peasants who had gone to other villages returned to pay their respects to the day and to those most pleasant valleys. Jesus explained to everyone how the vines were planted, how they were pruned, and how they were trained on canes which trembled in the wind. In short, no one went without wine. Everyone drank some, even the cardinal in the trees, and the snake that moves sadly among the rocks.

The ones who were opposed were the Judaic people of the

Jewish quarter. There at night they intoned litanies, they said, "We will follow God, we will show Him to you. Death comes from women."

Since the Jews in our village had brought syphilis, the boy babies were born crippled and lame, and the girl babies were idiots, without any sense. Our people grew tired of their laments, and the women said to Jesus:

"Master, they are infidels. They don't believe in the Prophet Macone. What are you waiting for to kill them?"

But Jesus of Nazareth said, "Never, never."

Even his companions, the apostles Francis, Peter, James, and Francis of Paola, said to the Master: "They are twisted people. They only know how to complain. What's keeping you from condemning them to eternal flames?"

This time the Master didn't reply, but looked at the white Jewish children with their eyes in shadows. Jesus, in truth, was thinking of making them into ordinary people, well-formed and graceful of intellect. Because of this his face became radiant. He stretched out his hands to work the miracle, the tips of his fingers sparkled. The people who were watching said, "Oh what a beautiful fire is being born!"

But nothing happened. The crippled stayed crippled; the old stayed old. His companions, the apostles, became frightened. They felt a great fear. "And can it be," they thought, "that the Master doesn't know how to perform the miracle?"

Then Jesus said the magic words, he wanted to try it another way. The little street echoed with a plaintive murmur, nothing happened.

"Master," shouted Peter, James, and Francis, "they are most pathetic beings, like swarming maggots. Do you really want to make men out of them? You won't succeed, you will never succeed."

Above, towards the Eastern sector, the Saracens were saying, "Master, syphilis has destroyed them. Make them all die, at least out of their bones we can make coal for the winter."

And winter in our village stings, as you know. The rook freezes up inside, and the grain in the fields and in the valleys freezes in stiff rows.

The apostles egged him on: "Make our brother Saracens happy. You'll get money from them; from these others, no."

Jesus had a thought, he thought: "They are lame, paralyzed. They will never be whole. At least as dead men they will be of use to my people."

He made a decision. He felt sorry for the Jewish babies, with their stumps of hands, and their eyes closed in endless silence.

With two fingers, the Master began to touch the foreheads of the Hebrews.

First a girl, then a woman or a baby with very beautiful hair. They fell down stone dead, they didn't have time to mourn the flower of their life. There were a thousand and one in all; it was a real slaughter. A sin, a great sin to kill human flesh. The old ones rolled into corners. The setting sun lit up their throats. A woman cursed God: "Adonài, Adonài, may the fire burn you." The young ones were like bare, rotten branches. Enough; let's not talk about it anymore.

They say that our people burned those Jewish bones in the raw winter that goes from riverbank to riverbank spinning fog and rain. Those flames were clear and singing against the grey sky. O divine intellect of Jesus!

The bodies of the Hebrews were turned into cinders, warm and shining. In the immense universe it was a tiny thing. When at night the owl hooted and the wind carried the sound of the hour, Jesus, helped by his Saracen brothers, sprinkled those ashes over the knolls, in the ravines. By day they shone white as seeds. In those lands the almond trees flourished, in flower they looked like a sea of mist. Birds, bees, and lizards came. It is said that no one could eat those almonds. They were of so bitter a bitterness that they weren't pleasing to the taste.

The people in our village weren't happy. They felt an endless sorrow. The women, to free their hearts, waited for the rising of the Moon from the beautiful East where there was no day. The Moon, that great lady, rose from the valley of Catalfaro. She stood beneath the people, and was as far from the earth as the earth from the sky. The mothers prayed:

> *Moon, dear Moon,*
> *Give us strength and bread,*
> *Bees, honey, and wool,*
> *O Moon, dear Moon, for you are as beautiful*
> *As a round loaf of bread.*

Jesus was overcome with sadness, he walked alone. He seemed aged with the age of the world. The women, to see him happy, had made him a staircase of silk, embroidered in gold, just like the one on which the dead of our village of Minèo climb at night onto the balconies.

"Jesus," they said to him, "don't be discouraged, you're young, you're handsome. Why don't you have any spirit and spark?"

On this staircase he descended to the moon that went walking below him as white as a young bride in May. Jesus arrived on the moon. As he walked, he left his footprints there. You could see that it was a slow walk, like that of an old man who is bent over with years. From the windows the women called out in loud, trembling voices, "Don't leave us, Jesus."

Poor child, the heaviness of his body was great. Above, you could see the earth burning. At night, the Saracen mothers loudly sang lullabies to their children, but they meant them for Jesus to hear:

> *O son of pearls, o desperate son,*
> *Your mind is crystal, up here the cock will crow,*
> *Your life is spent in wandering,*
> *You will have not palm fronds, but death.*

Meanwhile Orlando happened to pass through our land, with his son Orlandino. They were pursuing the divine mystery of life.

He asked a woman with beautiful hair, among pots of basil at the window, "My lady Saracen, where is Jesus?"

She didn't want to tell him. She could see that the knight-errant was troubled, for his eyes were shining.

"O good knight who goes through stony lands and dark woods, Jesus is to be found on the moon."

"What are you saying, my Lady? Your heart is crazed."

"On the moon, yes."

And she pointed it out to him. He looked and was astonished to see the moon, all lily and violets, descend into the depths.

"Can it be that Jesus is down there?"

So... Orlando found the silken stairway, he climbed down, followed by Orlandino, also in armor, with a little Durendal at his side. The earth above became more distant in a shadowy veil. "O Jesus," called Orlando. "My friend and master!"

The Paladin went from stone to brightly shining stone, while on the opposite side everything was black.

"What is the moon made of, father?" asked Orlandino.

They found Jesus seated under the quince tree planted by St. Francis of Paola. Jesus kissed Orlando, Orlando kissed Jesus. It was a moving scene.

"Are you also sad?" uttered Jesus.

Orlando remained with his eyes lost in that milky sea.

The knight wished to say that Jesus was God, lucky him, but the Angel Michael Gabriel spoke in a thin thread of a voice:

> In truth, in the eyes of God
> Jesus is like Adam. God
> Created him out of dust, then he said to him
> "Be." And he was.

Orlando looked at the Angel. He didn't answer. One can't argue with beings made of fleeting shadows. The two friends remained there for a day in the sweet light which in turns, in spurts, in leaps, passed through the vault of heaven. Then, they climbed up again.

Orlando went first, his Durendal clanging against the silken stairway.

Up here, the rich people and the poor people were waiting for him.

"What have you to say to us, Master? Do you still have a sorrowing voice?"

"What did you think about down there on the wandering moon?"

"Are you rested?"

They sat down on the rocks of the Walls. There were so many amidst the nettle and the mallow.

In the fields the peasants were working. Jesus said that he had meditated upon God.

"And who is God?" asked a woman with a black shawl on her head.

"Isn't he your father?" asked a child.

And an old man: "He is like the bird that is born from the egg. He is above us. He gives neither pleasure nor benefice."

Jesus smiled, he remembered his sheep-mother, his lady-mother, who sang:

Lullaby, how beautiful is
This child whom I hope will become a monk!
Lullaby, my heart is breaking,
The mother who nurses you with her own milk
Loves you with a true love and does not deceive you.

And he said: "God is neither father, nor mother, nor spirit with a bright-red halo."

The peasant men and women, who had come back at the news of the return of the Nazarene, were listening, along with the dogs, cocks, and birds. He was saying that once upon a time God did not exist, that there was the air and water and the void. He formed himself afterwards, but so little that not even the ants could see him. He was a grain of salt.

"Ooh," said the commonfolk. "He was a grain of salt!"

He did not grow suddenly like a day without an eclipse. He was not courageous, he was smitten with fear. It worried him if he saw even female seeds, sea waves. Thus spoke Jesus. He got bigger little by little, like bread being softened in milk. He absorbed the flares of the sun, and discolored lunar vapors. So... It's a story, my child. An old woman asked Jesus. "What are you making up, our rascal lily child?"

He went on. He said that in a ball there's something like a triangle where you can discover what is dead, what is living, what will happen in the centuries to come. Out of that point time is born, time which, like a coursing river, runs between the banks of the world. To understand it we have to free ourselves from our bodies of mortal clay.

Jesus did not stop. He felt like a brother to the blue sky, to the fiery steed, to the fish in the wave, to the beautiful young maiden. For Jesus, nephew of Michael Gabriel the cobbler, God is a lodestone: he attracts and repels things, he has neither feelings, nor breath, nor joy.

Growing larger in the air, after he had created himself, he turned himself into a sphere, good and round he rolled on his tortured path. He shaped the moons that moved along silently. He shaped the white and graceful star, even the Dog-Star bowed down. Around him he made a curve, as curved as the corolla of the pimpernel flower. That same God then gave birth to a female goddess like the light of a bright halo. Many gods were born: some of average size, some tiny, others even tinier, all frowning and troubled they entered into their own objects.

"Oh," said the same old woman, "are you trying to make fun of us, Jesus, our rose petal and deep thought?"

Those very gods turned around, created the winter, spring, but they were all fearful — their Father had passed it down to them. That fear-force dragged them down, and they shouted: "*In manibus tuis, in manibus tuis.*" But they could not stop the treacherous swelling. They plunged into the sea of things. Long, long threads held them together with beads of strong fear. They were united in fear. They shouted from terror, devoid of knowledge or divine virtue. They dissolved into sparks. They left in the air behind them hooves, breastplates, eyes, wings, feathers, and dust in great splendor. But they were dying: first God the Father, then God the Son, then the female goddesses, and their daughters. They became simply a flame in the midst of the stars. As one died, another would be born. It curled up in smoke, there was a murmur, a thread. The goddesses curled up into themselves, just so many little crying spirits. Thus spoke Jesus. So be it. The fable is ended.

St. Peter Plays the Violin, St. John Plays the Trumpet, and Jesus Destroys the World

*O*ften a bad year would come to our village, and then in November it wouldn't rain, in December it wouldn't rain, and in January the sun would shine in a thousand sparks. The countryside cried. Stunted grain would sprout up. The delicate bank of the river died. The women, dressed in black, would remain closed up in their houses with their shawls over their heads. Even the villagers in their home village knew they were damned.

Once Jesus happened to learn of the bad year. He had gone off with his companions the holy apostles – all of them with their eyes cast down – to forget himself. But a village woman said to him: "Jesus, are you asleep? Are you trying to find yourself? Don't you know that a bad year is upon our land, and that babies are dying?"

In fact, the poor children had neither bread, nor beans, nor onions. They were dying, one after another. The sad days went by like flashes of lightning. Evening hurled itself into day. There was a coming and going to the cemetery. At that time it was the custom to cast the dead into a huge, underground common grave. Everyone drank together of death, there was no escape.

"O woman," said Jesus, "I will leave my thoughts behind and I will come. Which is the path?"

And he went, walking through the underbrush. He felt the pain of love in his heart. Peter, James, and John, his companions who preached to the soft clouds, followed him.

But let's leave the clouds that had no water, and let's leave Jesus on the path that rose up toward the village. Here the villagers, in the midst of the barren fields, the women with spindles in their hands, thought of their dead ones. They felt them in their hands and in their eyes. In this way they learned to understand each other, those up here and those down there. At night the dead came up out of their communal grave. The darkness was an unsettling cloud.

The dead walked, each one carrying on his shoulders a pitcher full of tears. On their breasts sat sorrow.

The children, the little babies, newly dead, came in a row. The hazy star of Ursa Major illuminated them.

Their families, in festive dress, waited for them behind the windows, or they set candles at the doorways. The departed dead retained the memory of their children, their mothers, the donkey, the grass, the courtly knight-errant. The living, to assist them, placed silken stairways at their balconies, at the windows: in this way the dead climbed up, if they wished, pulling themselves up with the silver rings placed on the rungs. The poor things, they had thin bones and pallid nails. The living, as you know, watched them in hiding. Their hearts were tearful, the mothers because they were so happy, seeing their dead children wrapped in their white sheets. They were freed from the pains they had suffered, and from the fear of dark, shadowy death that played like a reed-pipe in their hearts. The young girls, in that deathly departure, were always twenty years old; the children were lilies without the heat of the sun. All of them, crying, sang voicelessly. They were the most delicate of creatures. Some were graceful and quivering, others looked for shining grains of wheat in the midst of the earth.

Let's go back to Jesus, who arrived in the still of the night.

"Aah, ooh," went St. Peter, "what's this? In this village the dead walk around in the streets?"

Even Jesus said, "Can this be? Have they left the asphodel fields and the purple mantle of God my Father?" They watched. Jesus gave it some thought and said to the sorrowing departed dead: "Go away, go away, this is no place for you!"

The dawn rose with a flower in its mouth. They faded away, and Jesus ordered them to go to the huge grave called Hades.

They went away, the poor beautiful souls, through shafts dug one inside the other. They found themselves in the asphodel plain from which one nevermore returns.

Afterwards, the living, up here, wanted to sound trumpets and wind-filled horns at night to call back their children and bring them back to the clear light of the stars and the purple grass.

But they could no longer rise up. They stayed down there in Hades along the banks of gray rivers. Down there the birds were broken, with black wings, and the crocuses were blue. With minds that were fading, oh, our dear children, they trampled frozen forest foliage.

Enough. Our people fell into a state of depression. They saw no one.

So St. Francis of Paola said to Jesus: "Master, what have you done? Don't the dead come any longer to this village of ours? The people are very unhappy. Don't you see? Don't you feel it?" Jesus hid himself in the olive grove. He cried, and only the Angel saw him. In Minèo the women wanted to set candles at the window, set unleavened bread in the baskets, set carpets fluttering, and to have the priests ring the bells! The departed were no longer able to rise up out of the infernal abyss of Hades. They heard only from afar the peal of the bells.

Now Jesus, on the advice of John, the friend with whom he had shared the tranquil sea, the forest, the meadow, what did he do? He said that it was time to form a band to play in the village and bring back festivity and laughter.

Peter had a violin, and John a euphonium on which he played airs and cavatinas. Master Jesus the Nazarene, nephew of Michael Gabriel, played the bombardon. The sound traveled through streets, lanes, and alleys, and passed over the enamored salamander. The children who were not dead lessened their hunger by following behind Jesus. The carters, the carpenters, the potters, and Magdalene, mother of Giufà, were happy. The goldfinch flew in beautiful song.

Everyone felt different. No one thought any longer of the lost dead. The old people were in ecstasy with such music in their hearts.

Once there was an eclipse of the moon, and with the earth covering the moon down there in the very deep valley, the people became frightened. The band, playing the euphonium, the trumpet, and the violin, made it shine again, this moon that again ate up the stars. As you see, it seemed a most beautiful life, and little thought was given to the great famine. Jesus and his friends the holy companions even climbed up on the roofs to play, and the cocks and birds in the bare grillwork of leaves answered them. People from every village hurried forth.

"Haven't you heard? Jesus has formed a band!"

"Is this possible?"

"Yes, it's possible! Everything is possible!"

"Only nothing is not possible!"

There was joy and passion, but the priests informed the Pope, who thought it over on his golden throne.

"Can it be that Jesus plays the bombardon?" he said.

"Yes, Your Holiness. That's how it is."

The matter did not please the Pope.

"Can all this be happening in my realm? And who am I? The least of sovereigns?"

The priests kept at him: "There's no religion anymore, Your Holiness! No one comes to church anymore. They are all Saracens!"

The Pope thought to call King Frederick, who was enjoying himself by the sea, in a land that was not Sicily. He was corrupting his soul with ancient words.

"Majesty, King Frederick, His Holiness wishes to speak to you."

So off went Frederick, with his mandola and his trusty steed.

"I do not wish to return to Sicily ever again," said the King.

"You must return there with your army. Jesus is turning everyone into Saracens, in adoration of the God Macone."

The Pope was the Pope, so Frederick reluctantly agreed. The army of the Normans came – horses, knights with swords and resounding guns. Our island was crowded with them. The earth trembled.

"Run away, Jesus!" the children said to him when they saw the army near Carratabbìa, making its way through the smoking paths.

St. Joachim, who was the simplest and most pure, said, "Jesus, let's allow ourselves to be arrested. We have sinned."

"Arrested?" St. Peter said angrily. "By those infidel Christians? Never."

They went down into the valley under Mt. Catalfaro. The soldiers of the King made their way up into our village. The people shut themselves inside. No one wanted to know anything about King Frederick. They longed for Giufà.

"He's the one we need! Him!"

The army drew up on the mountain. The King, sighting Jesus down there, looking like a small bird in an immense shadow, said: "Hurl stones down upon that one!"

They hurled down tiny little stones, small, big, and huge boulders. They were shiny and very hot because of the glaring red sun. One stone, two, one hundred, one thousand, one thousand and one: an avalanche that came down in a loud thundering. Jesus was slightly advanced in age. He was getting old like everything in the world. No science could help him. His holy companions said to him: "Jump here. Jump there. Get down. Hang onto that olive tree."

They all jumped to protect themselves and not be crushed. The echo went from olive tree to olive tree, from almond tree to almond tree. The stones rolled in the dust, among uprooted bushes, among clumps of earth. Jesus, poor unfortunate child, jumped. He didn't stay still for an instant.

As God willed, it ended. Evening came to the rocks, to the yellow grass, tired from being beaten down. Dark night came. Jesus was saved along with his holy companions the apostles.

Joachim as usual said that they should form another band, this time with swords, trusty steeds, and bombs.

"You want us to become bandits?" sighed St. Peter.

Jesus said, "How can this be? If we were to hurl a stone at every dog that barks we would wear out our arms."

And Joachim: "Jesus, let us become bandits. It is the best idea at this point."

"Never, never, Joachim."

Jesus had sad eyes, like a man under a spell. He was not happy. The unhappiness of the past ate away at him. His meekness was transformed into anger. John made him julep and rosolio.

"Drink, drink, it will clear your thoughts."

But his rancor remained. In his heart he felt an aversion to mankind. He didn't sleep for seven nights, then he felt weak. He couldn't see the reddish olives fall from the trees.

In an outburst he said:

"You know what I say?"

"What do you say, Master?"

"I am going to destroy the world."

"You want to destroy the world?"

"Who thinks any longer of the lights that illumine the evening, of the donkey Rondello, of the bread fresh out of the oven, of the cricket that sang?"

The apostles in chorus: "O bitter life! What is to be done?"

"Who thinks any longer of their mother's song, of the bed made of straw, of the grain of wheat?"

"O sinful life! O destiny!"

"Who thinks of their Father, dead from a blood clot, of the holy moon that shines in the hollows?"

"O sinful earth!"

Jesus grew old. There was not light in his eyes but little sparks. A certain energy took hold of him: his mind sparkled. The olive tree obeyed him, it bent down its gray branch.

He was sad, more so than in the past, and he felt the black water of evil in his mind. He was not happy either with himself or with mankind. So, what did he do then? He destroyed everything completely – he destroyed trees, rivers, the dew and the rays. That land split open, it broke into pieces, everything was dust. It remained a huge ditch with the inhabitants dead at the bottom among the precious stones.

"Oh, what are you doing?" cried Joachim. And Peter: "This is not the law of God Macone, our Father and Lord!"

Jesus did not reply. The dark water rose up within him. Then it was America's turn, which fell through the burning air into a parched abyss. The villagers who threshed on the threshing-floor, turning along with the treading hooves of their donkeys, spoke. They said:

"O God, what is this deviltry? The world is breaking into fragments! The stars are falling headlong!"

Evil destiny! Even the villages near us – Palagonia, Scordia, Grammichele, Vizzini, Licodia Eubea – broke, split, fell into caves and wells. The hens flapped their wings. The children asked themselves: "Is the whole world coming apart?"

The cry of the olive trees was heard. The reeds and stalks bent down. Everything around our village was dark, revealing an abyss.

"O Jesus, our ruin!" shouted the villagers. "O beautiful St. Agrippina!"

Giufà, who was sleeping happily under a carob tree where our lands border with those of Militello, was saved. The roots remained firmly rooted in the clods and clumps of earth. He was able to pull himself out of the abyss that drank up the last plaintive light. Still alive was Eumeo the swineherd, who kept a hut and pigs at Camùti, where Jesus retired, undone, like a jasmine without leaves. The nymphs saw him pass, and the shepherds made the sign of the holy cross.

Eumeo the swineherd friend asked, "Has Jesus destroyed the world? Is even our Odysseus dead?"

Jesus made the sign of the cross. He said: "It is finished. No one can persecute us now." Eumeo, who was gentle and faithful, cried, but seeing the rocks burst into flames, said, "Enough. Let's eat."

He killed a small suckling pig. He seasoned it, set among the laurel burning in the flames, with fragrant onion, with fragrant garlic, with pepper and cheese.

"Eat, eat!"

St. Peter, St. John, St. Joachim, St. Francis also ate. Outside it stormed. There was thunder and lightning. They were all old, those holy men. After the meal, their hearts were heavy. They slept leaning against each other's shoulders. There was heavy thunder and lightning.

When it was day, Jesus remembered his deed, and he felt sadder seeing only our village in all that black land, and the torrent of water without song in the valley.

After three months and three days, Jesus could see no longer, he had lost his sight. He dragged his feet, old age ran after him like a dark horse. He shouted:

"Women, give me some light."

He could no longer manage to perform miracles. Electricity rose up and sparkled in his hands, but his mind remained a blank. He couldn't perform any real act. He went groping along the streets where, because of the burning sun, old people slept on straw in the street where the roof tiles gave off a little shade. His companions the apostles were not always able to follow him. They would fall asleep with a whispering of breath, the poor, tired old men.

Giufà recalled the past, his friend Jesus, and he looked for him. Once he saw Orlando, white of hair, still disdained by Angelica, that treacherous woman. He was carrying Durendal at his side and was wearing his cuirass, but he had no desires, for time passes like a perennial river that wipes out the rose, the lily, and memory.

"O Orlando!" said Giufà. "Are you here too? You were saved?"

Orlando smiled. He recognized Giufà, and embraced him. Durendal rang on the stones. St. Peter was happy when he saw him. "Come," he said to him. And he took him to Jesus who, being an old man, 108 years old, was hardly able to recognize him, as he meanwhile prophesied thus:

"Nothing can be known, and even if it is known, it is not understood. Who can know the Truth? And if it is known, it cannot be explained."

The children, who had lost their memory of Jesus, shouted at him, "Hey, old Gorgias, what are you saying? Have you lost your mind?"

But Orlando, the paladin of France, to keep those mocking kids at a distance, blew his horn that resounded in the vines, the valleys, and the houses. The old women humbly said to him, "O, old man, would you like bread and onions?"

The little children asked with stammering tongues: "Hey, who are you that you eat and sleep in our village?"

So... Meanwhile people were dying. There was no escape from the beautiful stretch of ancient lands sunken into the sea that in the unceasing light pounded against the abyss. The tailors died. The shoemakers died. The water-vendor died. The cricket died without song, and the potters without clay. The tinsmiths died. The sparrow that found itself under silent stars died. The farmer Angelo Mangiapicca died. Our village was a black diamond in the infinite sky. Seventeen old men, thirty-three women, and eleven children were left. That's how the world was.

Jesus was sleeping in a stall near the donkey Rondello, and that's where Giufà found him. He was wearing only one sock, with red and white stripes. With him was Michael of the Order of Discalced Michelines.

"O Nazarene, are you always asleep? It's Giufà. Wake up."

"O my dear Giufà!"

"Come with me. What are you doing here all by yourself like a fool?"

The old Nazarene moved through the streets with death seated on one shoulder. He couldn't say anything. He was trembling with fear, just as he did when he was calm. At the top of the main street Don Mario Gagliano kept his tavern open because he was thinking of the resurrection of the dead. His wife, head bowed, was deftly sewing a veil of yellow lace.

"It will be useful for us dead ones!"

"You only ever think of one thing, for crying out loud."

The tin weathervanes turned in perpetual motion on the roof where the wind passed. Don Mario invited them in to drink a glass.

"Drink, drink."

"It's good," said Jesus, and he licked his lips.

"I don't like wine, but water from the streams," remarked Giufà, who was watching the cloudy shadows descend over the eaves of the roof.

Orlando drank with his lips curled, his eyes slowly turning at the sounds of the north wind.

Sometimes that poor old dying Jesus the Nazarene, to thank Don Mario Gagliano, wanted to turn the water into wine. Yes, his hands sparkled, but the spark was immediately extinguished. He couldn't work the miracle. The old women of the village contemplated the endless rain. In communal litany they sang: "Jesus, our own, save us from plagues and storms."

Enough. Let's leave Jesus, Giufà, Don Mario Gagliano, and Orlando the knight, as old age walked over their sleeping hands and a thousand rains came to Minèo – and here let's end the fable. Amen.

The Death of Jesus

The story is told that light came forth from the abyss, reshaping little by little the lost world. Dark Africa rose again. America recovered its woods and valleys. Male and female, the people were reborn.

"Oh," they said in our village, "the earth is being re-formed."

The cornel tree stood in the ravines, the cornflower was on the plains. But the earth was sodden. You only had to set your foot down to see the clumps of earth, the shrub, the olive tree, sink back again.

The soldiers ran to the Pope.

"Your Holiness, Your Holiness, are you still sleeping?"

"Oh, what's the matter, my sons?"

"The earth is reflowering, the bird is returning to its ancient nest. And Jesus is still alive."

"Jesus still alive? Can this be? Ay!"

The Pope wrote immediately, artfully, to King Frederick.

"O Majesty and King, in your kingdom, the life of Jesus still goes on."

"O Holiness and Celestial Word," Frederick replied, "I am giving the order to capture our proud enemy immediately."

It took the army a year, a month, and a day to arrive in our village. The earth slid out from under their feet, leaving puddles that reflected stars like rubies. An old farmer came running. He said to the Nazarene:

"Are you the Nazarene, Our Lord, Son of God Macone? Escape if you are, for the trot of the horses can be heard."

That scoundrel King Frederick said to the people, "I bring you bread and onions and fava beans."

Everyone awaited the King with guitars and mandolins. Jesus, aided by his brothers and companions, the apostles, hid himself in the cave in Mt. Carratabbìa. But a Norman soldier spotted him. Jesus was sleeping when they seized him. Giufà was sleeping next to him. They chained Giufà up first, for they were afraid of his incredible strength. "What's happening?" said Giufà, his eyes burning red.

But what could he do? By then he was covered in chains.

Then they chained up Jesus, hand and foot, poor beautiful child.

Orlando was walking all alone, he was thinking of the enchanted Ardennes. They threw a cloud of tar in his face. They covered him with a silken sheet. They bound him hand and foot with silver chains.

They people learned of it, and they wanted to rebel.

"They've taken someone called Jesus."

"Jesus the miraculous? The lily son?"

"That's him!"

"O God!"

"To arms, to arms!"

But what could they do against an army that made use of bombards, arrows, and sublime fervor?

"Take the Saracen Jesus to the castle!" ordered His Majesty King Frederick.

He was shut in there for three days and three nights. The horned owl didn't sing. The swallow flew away. Frederick had a thought – do you know what it was? On the esplanade of the castle were three olive trees – one to the west where the sun dies, and one to the east where the star rises. The third faced the north wind.

"O soldiers, o captains," said the King, "these olive trees have open branches like horns. Hang our three proud enemies on the cross there."

A captain said, "Majesty, but what will His Holiness think of this?"

The Pope made known his thought by a messenger, swift as lightning.

"King Frederick, my friend and shield of Christianity, scourge Jesus, destroyer of the world. He has made the rich poor, and the poor rich. Perhaps putting him on the cross is the just punishment."

And so it was done.

"Women," said the Saracen peasants, "at the castle they are putting Jesus our brother and Lord on the cross. The same end awaits Giufà and Orlando. Who will soothe our hearts?"

But no one soothed their hearts. July was burning. At night, because of the stifling darkness, you couldn't even see Ursa Major or Ursa Minor. Anyway... The mother of Jesus, Lady Maria, learned of it. She ran to the castle. She knocked at the great iron gate that clanked.

"Knock, knock."

"Who's there behind these doors?" said the soldiers.

Jesus, already on the cross with his head turned toward the smoke of the east:

"Perhaps it is my unfortunate mother."

And she:

> Child of the black forehead,
> My ardent beauty,
> Dawn in the star's ray,
> Oh, who tortures and afflicts you?

Jesus uttered some words. They could barely be heard. The breeze of the valley scattered them over the slope:

> Mother, blood of my blood, I
> cannot speak. The King
> has taken away my golden crown,
> and has pressed upon me a crown of thorns.

And his mother, with a shudder, said:

Use little nails of silk,
for they must pass through divine flesh.

And the soldiers, with a great murmuring, like fronds:

No, Our Mother, we must use blunt nails.
This is the order we have received.
Your son is passing into a dark life.
We cannot help him, o sorrowful lady!

In the village – buzz, buzz – they learned of it.
"They are killing Jesus!"
"They are killing Jesus."

The people climbed slowly to the castle heights, where the wind whistled in the breeze of the sorrowful valley. The children were in tears. They played "truoccole," carrying in their hands flat pieces of wood that they struck with a little bronze hammer. The bells were rung by the people. In the silence they sounded the sorrow of the finite world. The soldiers put Jesus on the cross facing the east where the shining sun rises, Orlando facing west where the day burns in its ending, and Giufà facing north. The women were singing. It sounded like a lullaby:

O our dear little tortured lily child,
our beautiful fable, cool bank and river,
Death tears at you, rends you,
Oh, our joyous child.

The women circled the castle with lit candles. In the valleys and on the heights, the goatherders drew figures of catnip, mallow, and mayflowers on the ground.

Many things gathered on the esplanade of the castle: the feather of the dying swallow, the hen, the lamb without grass, and the donkey Rondello, who brayed at the hills, meadow, and the woods. The hot stone fell from the roof. The pig arrived. The sound of the clock in the tower arrived. The poor arrived, together with the dark evening:

There was Turi the artichoke,
Cicciu the dogpisser,
Ianu the matchstick,
and Puddu the hunchback,
Peppi the doorpost
and Matteu the oil vendor,
and Antoniu the asparagus-sucker
and Angiuzzu the chicory vendor.

To the west, where the sun set plaintively, Orlandino, accompanied by guitar players, mourned for his father:

O father Orlando, we are here in great chorus;
Twisted in sorrow, we send up a song.
You are the World, you are the Pure One, the Sound One.
In your hand you hold Durendal, but your true
calling, o dear father, is joyous love.

The castle shuddered with voices, the women's tresses curled in sorrow. Mother Magdalene said:

Giufà, dear son, I gave you milk,
I loved you with a true love and do not deceive you;
Give form, my son, and luminous chastity
to the water of the river, to our holy heaven.

The striking of the hammers could be heard. They drove in the nails. The knight Orlando, dressed in iron, could not breathe. He heard his son playing, and he thought: "O my son Orlandino, beloved fire, beauty and strength pass away into Nothingness."

Giufà was writhing, the nails were too big for his hands. Oh, what pangs, our poor child Giufà! He was sweating. Even the rocks were sweating. One rolled back. The sun was fleeing, fleeing was the sun. The last rays beat down on the face of Giufà, who did not cry, did not give way, even though his body was beset by tempests.

Then came Jesus' turn. The soldiers came to him. His mother said:

> Nail him with a little nail of silk
> for my son is of divine flesh.
> Should he fall slowly, slowly, into the black well
> the day will draw him forth no more!

All the people were in tears, as the sun set in the infinite silence. Jesus, his forehead crowned with thorns, trembled all over. Here everyone heard him:

> Mother, dearest Mother, I am sore afraid.
> In my soul there is no peace.
> Free me from the cross and from the world.
> Dearest Mother, I am afraid, my body is trembling.
> You must convey my pain to the grass,
> to the colors of this last sky.
> I am suffering from the loss of my senses.

His mother, in the clearing, beat her breast. She drew out her white and flaccid breasts:

> Son, dearest son, with these breasts
> I gave you milk, and she who nurses you
> with her own milk does not deceive you.
> You ascended the cross grieving, disconsolate,
> without physician. You brought freshness to my womb,
> most splendid light. But no more.
> Stay here with me: row, row
> in life. I will yet give you milk,
> my divine child, ruler of the world.

There was a weeping. All the women pulled their black shawls over their heads. To comfort the mother, Ciccio the matchstick played the cornet, Matteu the oil-vendor sweetly played the violin, and Angiuzzu beat cymbals together to make the light of the dying sun grow stronger.

The king in the castle gave the order in a loud voice: "Let loose the falcons. Let them fly, for they must suck the life from the heads of the three condemned men."

There were one hundred and one falcons, of a wondrous beauty in both plumage and daring. The captains held them with one hand, using long cords of golden linen. It was a spectacle to behold. The moles fled. The crickets fled. The birds took off into the clear sky. The kites, circling in the sky, understood that they were to swoop down to the terrace of the castle. The soldiers had taken off Orlando's helmet, poor knight-errant. His old, white hair shone in the sun. A falcon with red plumage struck him in the forehead with his beak. Those birds, rapacious kites, swooped down, one after the other. Flying straight down, they struck the knight. Orlandino heard the attacks. They were sharp blows. Matthew played his violin more sweetly. St. Peter played the euphonium – the poor holy man was crying.

Orlando's pierced brain quivered. Blood and feelings flowed forth. Jesus felt in his eyes that the golden veil of his life was lifting. He screamed. He cried out. He had always been afraid, that man. At night he even dreamed, in horror, of fear.

> O Mother, dearest Mother, the world grows dark before me.
> The olive tree dances before me. Oh, what
> shall I do, Mother? There is an abscess on my neck.
> I feel my tongue grow numb. They are pecking,
> they are pecking at my brain. Who is doing it?
> O dear lost mother, I am terribly frightened!
> Don't let me die, Mother. I desire light
> but I hold the whole world within my flesh

in blood! Dearest, dearest Mother, I am dying
in fear. It is a black lake.
They are tearing my brain to pieces.
I am infinitely afraid,
I can no longer hold onto Time, which you, Mother,
gave me with the milk from your breasts.

Angiuzzo played on. St. Peter played on. Gioacchino played. St. Francis played. Even in the shadows of the ditches their words were heard:

O Jesus of Nazareth, there only remain to us the hills,
the rivers, the ruby sun, and your holy burial.
Oh, blessed one, for you are going to the beautiful
meadow of death, where there is no languishing,
nor is there sickness, nor poverty, nor sorrow.

The falcons continued to fly upward. They plunged down again, not sated with blood and brains. Jesus, with a voice grown faint, was dying.

Mother of my memory, unfortunate Mother,
I am terribly afraid. It is an
earthquake, Mother, that makes me pale, takes me
where there is Nothing. Mother, give me milk from
your breasts that do not deceive.

A stone was shining in the last ray of the sun that was setting in whiteness over Mt. Catalfaro. The great King Frederick, our Master, was enjoying the sight from the tower. He said, "Our Dominion remains that of the six senses: taste, touch, smell, the Eye, the Ear that hears the cock crow and the leaves rustle, the sense of Death that passes over the olive tree and the stream." On the olive tree those poor tormented children were dying, were mourning their fleeing spirit. The petals turned to ashes. The mountains of Coste were covered in ashes. Jesus died with blood on his dark forehead. Giufà had one large tear in his eye. Orlando sounded like a guitar of death, like the distant song of the owl.

The people cried out, "O Our Trinity, Jesus-Giufà-Orlando, you are going into the dark grave. The world will be no more."

All the animals of the world came: the cow without horns, the cat black as coal, the finch with folded wings, the piglet and the pig (even the pig was there!), and the hen. The fava bean flowered. The donkey Rondello was there. The heavenly dove was there. Jesus died like a bird with his mouth open. His thoughts sank into the black sea. Giufà alone remained, falling into the Nothingness announced by the soldiers' blast. In death, Orlando felt himself grow large, swelling over promontories and cliffs.

It grew dark. Evening came sweetly. Frederick, under the golden lamps of the castle, felt that he was the noble lord who lords over the earth.

"You are the defender of our holy Christian religion," the notary said to him.

The fable ends here, there's no more to be said. We await the song of the beautiful sun. Jesus is no more.

Profane Stories

The Pig and Father Superior

One day there was a peasant who was always working and always hungry. He went to work in the country. His master owned a sow that had borne fourteen piglets, all of them fine and sleek, with their tails sticking up. So the master said to him, "Giuseppe, when these little pigs get bigger, I will give you one." Giuseppe was very happy, and he gazed at a shady young tree. That evening, when he returned home through the sun's rays and the rocks, he told his wife and children of the matter. In their great delight they began to dance.

After some months, his master said to him, "Listen, this evening I will give you the piglet." When it was evening, Giuseppe carried off the piglet, and he felt like a knight in all the splendor of his armor. He walked happily along many paths and jumped over rocks and stones. He had a thought. What did he think? He thought he would leave the piglet in the broad plain that belonged to the Josephite Capuchin monks of the Sacred Heart. There the piglet could eat all he wanted of cardoons, lupines, sainfoin, pimpernel, proud myrtle, and swaying white grass. He left the piglet.

When the pig got big – with buttocks like this! – Father Superior Don Fragalà, who had eyed this porker, said to the villager, "Leave it a while longer, it will get fatter and better."

He left it there. That piglet became a pig that was so big that no matter where you looked you could only see only fat. Then the farmer said to Father Superior Don Antonio Fragalà, "Are you going to give me the pig?" But he, in the cleverness of his mind, said, "No, this porker belongs to us, for we have raised it with blessed herbs."

Giuseppe felt a dark veil fall over his heart. He returned home as the sunset, with its blond tresses, was filling the countryside. So... When they heard what had happened, his wife and children began to cry. But Giuseppe said, "Stop, don't cry. I'll take care of this."

Then Father Fragalà of the Josephite Capuchin Franciscans fell sick, and the birds sang more thickly in the woods. Cheep, cheep, peep, peep. They learned of it in the village. Hearing of the matter, Giuseppe dressed himself up as a doctor, with a doctor's bag under his arm, a hat and cane. He began walking in the grassy plain below the convent – not very pleasant, given the hot sun. Leaning out a window sculpted with angels, a Josephite monk saw this doctor. He went in right away to tell Father Superior. "Father, there's a doctor down there. Shall we summon him for you?"

"Yes, call him. That way we'll know what this fever is that's cooking me like hell."

The monk went down into the plain. The singing grass smiled. The monk spoke up and asked, "Doctor, our Father Superior is burning with fever. In the name of Our Lord Jesus Christ, would you examine him?"

"Yes."

He went up through a dark staircase where he heard the clock sounding. It was saying, in a very gloomy tone: "Time is passing; our life is passing."

Father Superior offered the doctor a seat. He said, "Here I am, examine me."

"Listen," said Giuseppe, after he'd checked him over, "if you want to get well, you need the purple herb. You must have someone search for it."

Father Superior called the Josephite Capuchin brothers. They came. He said, "Go search for the purple herb."

They departed in humble obedience. Some went to the highest mountain, some to the dark valley, some along the dry riverbed. The doctor locked the door. He drew near to Father Superior, and with his cane gave him a savage thrashing, enough to turn him to coal and pitch. Father Superior shouted: "Help, help!"

Who could hear him in the deserted convent where day was dying? And he: "Help! The doctor is beating me!"

And Giuseppe: "Ha, ha! I'm not the doctor, but Giuseppe of the blessed pig. Give it to me." Giuseppe rained so many blows upon him that finally, after a long time, the Josephite Capuchin monks returned from the mountain and from the paths where the sun had died. They heard, "Help, help!" They ran, but the villager had already escaped. He covered the earth with his long legs.

"What's happening? What is it?" asked the monks.

"That fellow wasn't the doctor but the owner of the pig. Oh, oh, I'm dying."

"And so what are we supposed to do with this purple herb?"

It was an herb with red roots and a shining stem. The head of the flower shone like the sun.

"Throw it away. Throw it away! Call a real doctor."

This doctor came with a silver cane and a cravat. He said, "These were clubbings, and some of the best."

He gave him ointment of Magdalene. Father Superior got better, but the pig remained in the plain at the convent. Now the Josephite monks were thinking about killing it and making it into sausages, pork fat, and pork chops with fragrant smells. Father Superior Don Antonio Fragalà, all healed, gave the order to ring the bells. They rang high and low in the valley where the kite was wheeling over the withered breasts of the village women. The Catholic people, hearing the holy sound spread out over the roofs and vines and roads, said, "Let's go to church, because Father Superior is healed."

They filed out: children, women, and old people. They heard the cattle bells of the hornèd herd. After Mass, Father Superior began hearing the confessions of the faithful who had gathered with tears and prayers. Afterwards those Catholic people returned home, leaving the cemetery behind them on the ascent full of still cypresses. Only one penitent remained, a woman in great affliction. Father Superior said to her, "Come back tomorrow."

The woman replied, "Father, I have so many children, how can I leave the youngest tomorrow?" The monk replied, "Alright. Come into the confessional."

No one was in the church. Outside, in the eaves, the first sparrows of evening sang in mirth.

"I'm not a woman, but the one who owns the pig." Father Superior, imagining the clubbings again, said to him in a weak voice, "Leave me alone, leave me alone, in the name of Our Triune, omnipotent God."

"Never mind Triune and Diune. I want my pig."

The clubbings began. "Ay, ay, ay," cried Don Antonio. "Stop, stop, I'll give you the pig."

It was an enormous pig that – lucky thing – was like a ball, with white violets between its thighs. It was swollen with fat, even in its tail. When farmer Giuseppe returned to Minèo, his wife and children were extremely happy. (This is the story others call "Uncle Ménico Taccia's Pig." He was a cobbler.)

They had a feast. The people, smelling the aroma, said, "You're eating all by yourselves?" They had shut themselves up inside because of the great hunger they felt. They didn't even let the fumes go out into the little street, full of children and women who were hoping for a little bit of divine grace in the form of flesh. The moon, when it appeared on their roofs, laughed in its white vestment.

My story is told, my story is written. There they are with their stomachs full and rumbling, and here we are, dying of hunger.

The Tripe

Once there was a cobbler, small and thin, with no belly, who was called "Pays-his-debts" because his heart was honest and his feelings were true. His wife said to him: "I have a hankering for tripe." Outside was a winter that was coming down from the sky to the earth in a murmur of rain and sighs. Her husband replied: "I would like some tripe, too."

He went out, heading for Don Papé the butcher, in the town square where evening, along with the rain, was approaching. The wind that came from the valley, where there were olive and almond trees, wailed through the street.

He arrives at the butcher's. He goes in and says to Don Papé: "I'd like a kilo of pig's innards."

"Right away. I'll get it for you."

The pig was hanging from the hook in strips of red meat. It lit up the whole shop of Don Papé the good butcher.

He cuts it, weighs it with a kilo weight made of bronze, and hands over the beautiful pork tripe.

"Take it, it's yours."

Pays-his-debts hands over the money. He counted it out in silver coins – they were tiny little coins earned by the sweat of the poor cobbler's brow. He goes off. Along the main street, twisting up towards the churchyard of Santa Maria, there was no one and nothing but the wind. The doors were closed, the windows were closed, the donkeys didn't bray. Dying of hunger in the street were:

Ciccio the matchstick,
Matteo the oil vendor,
Cicciu the dogpisser,
Puddu the hunchback,

and there was Antoniu the asparagus sucker,
and Peppi the doorpost,
and Angiuzzu the chicory vendor.

"We're hungry," they said.

"So come and eat with me. I have tripe all wrapped up in my pocket."

And they went off. The wind was making its way through the street. The bell pealed.

"Father Fragalà is ringing for Mass," said Pays-his-debts. "Let's go to church to pray and give thanks to Our Lord God Macone for the pork tripe from Don Papé the butcher."

"Whatever you say," said his friends.

So they went. The priest Don Fragalà was preaching from the pulpit. He looked like an angel with a flaming sword. There were twelve women, an old man, and three children. Outside it was raining, and the water thundered on the roofs, making a smoky shadow. The priest said:

"Many sins are committed because of the belly. Everyone thinks of his belly, which is a hole that empties into hell."

At first Pays-his-debts resisted. In his pocket he clenched the paper bag that held the tripe. The poor people, kneeling, beat their breasts. The angels turned nice and quiet under the vault where cherubs holding extinguished candles were suspended. Ciccio the matchstick, Angiuzzu the chicory vendor, Peppi the doorpost, Matteu the oil vendor, and Ciccio the dogpisser all stamped their feet from the cold. The cold, you know, is an ugly beast that makes you cry hard tears.

The priest: "Mortal sins are committed because of the belly. There is no one who is saved."

Pays-his-debts muttered to himself: "The one time I buy a kilo of tripe and Don Fragalà decides to embarrass me in public."

"Hold out, hold out, dear friend," said Ciccio the matchstick, Matteu the oil vendor, Ciccio the dogpisser, in deferential silence to God.

But he couldn't hold out. He couldn't stand it. He takes the paper bag with the tripe and throws it in the priest's face.

"Here's your belly. *You* eat it: that way you'll wind up in the hellfire of your Triune God."

The priest grows frightened. Then he catches on. He picks up the fresh pork tripe and puts it in the pulpit. His preaching grew weak. It got fainter and fainter.

Bending down he said in a thin voice to Pays-his-debts, "Good for you, you must give drink to the thirsty and food to the hungry. Good for you, Pays-his-debts."

And Don Fragalà heard the harmonious pealing and the resounding trumpeting in his stomach. He finished his sermon quickly and rang the forlorn bell. The pealing was very faint. As soon as he got home, the priest took out a pot. He put in water, pepper, salt, curly fennel, basil, rue, and Hyblean thyme, and cooked it all up. O jubilation, O venerable sign! O happy soul that goes riding forth in Love.

Let's leave the priest Don Antonio Fragalà to his flashing tongue, and go to Pays-his-debts, who heads home with all his friends. One of them had only one shoe, another a torn jacket, another's socks were in tatters. The rings of rain grew thicker in the street. All of them rubbed their stomachs, where horses were galloping in a burst of sparks. His wife sees her husband coming and says, "And you're bringing with you all these starving guys?" And then, "Let the will of our God Diune and Triune Jesus Christ of Nazareth be done. Give me the tripe."

"The tripe?"

"Of course. I can't wait to cook and eat it."

"What tripe are you talking about?" he said unhappily.

"Well then, what happened? What didn't happen?"

"What happened is that I threw it in the face of Don Antonio Fragalà."

And he told her everything, pa-da-bum, pa-da-ba. His poor, famished, barefoot friends stood around him with the horses running wildly in their stomachs.

"Oh, that's just great!" said his wife. "Well done, my husband, you animal. And now what do we do?"

"Ah, shut up, or I'll break your face with a stick. I don't want to go to hell because of some tripe, and because of your beautiful face. If I were the wind, I'd blow you down."

His wife: "If I were fire, I'd burn you alive."

"Shut up! You know what they say to busybodies? Don't get mixed up in somebody else's affairs, don't interfere, no good deed goes unpunished."

His wife felt a wave of the stormy sea in her breast. Silently, silently, she bit her hands. His poor friends, worn out and hungry, said, "So, there's nothing to eat? What are we going to do?"

"This is what we're going to do," said the woman. "We're going to watch the rain that is frying the roofs like meat."

And the rain, with its long legs running through the olive trees, the almond trees, the ditches, like a fire it fried the world. And those poor fools stood there watching it and amusing themselves. This is how the story finishes. Here it is, there it is, and I am the wife of the ricotta-vendor.

The Pumpkin

A preacher was expected in our village. He was traveling on the back of his donkey through the fields and valleys where the grain was already growing amidst asphodel and red flowers. Evening came. It grew dark. The day was changing from bright to cloudy.

"Oh, it's raining!" the preacher said to himself, full of burning hunger.

There came thunder, lightning, flashes. The rain grew intense. He found himself in the Nunziata quarter, where there lived a farmer called "The Saracen," because he adored the rivers, the air, and the sun that rises and sets. The preacher, who was a Discalced Capuchin, knocked at the door of the Saracen's house.

"Who's there?"

"It's me."

"Who's me?"

"I am a priest of God who has lost the way and the light."

The Saracen opened the door. He let the preacher dry off in front of a beautiful fire of laughing olive wood. The poor room of the peasant was gleaming with bright waves.

"I have fava beans to eat."

"Let it be fava beans," said the Discalced Capuchin preacher. "Even they are creatures of our Crucified Lord."

"With olive oil and onions."

"Let it be onions."

The monk appeased his hunger. Now he felt as transparent as a nymph.

"I have hay to sleep on."

"Let it be hay! It comes from grain."

They slept together next to the donkey of the Saracen and the donkey of the monk. The peasant woke up before daylight. The storm was over. The shores of the earth were still dark. The Saracen dressed himself in the dark to go into town. He made a mistake and put on the monk's tunic. The beautiful dawn was still far off. Off he went on his donkey.

When he got to town, he saw a huge crowd of good Christian folk silhouetted against the light of the coming day. Upon seeing him, they shot off firecrackers, Roman candles, and sparklers. Lots of festive fireworks went off. The rascal Saracen peasant realized their mistake. It made his spirit rejoice, and his soul rang out in full peal.

"Hurray for the preacher of Our Lord!"

"Hurray!"

"Hurray!"

A priest came up to him, Don Antonio Fragalà, with his three-cornered hat on his head. He said to him: "Welcome, brother in Christ. Let us go into the Church."

Behind them came the people, men and women and little children. But on the way the Saracen said to the priest Don Antonio: "I am not a preacher."

"Can this be? Who are you?"

"There's been a mistake. God willed it."

And he told him about everything – the storm, the beans, and the Discalced preacher.

"May our Lord and Savior's will be done," said the priest. "Don't be frightened." (The Saracen laughed in his heart.) "Climb up into the pulpit with me and say whatever I tell you."

In the meantime, the real preacher arrived in the peasant's clothing, but everyone recognized it as the clothing of a Saracen. At that time it was customary to crucify a Saracen peasant, just as Jesus had been crucified.

"And who better than this solitary farmer?" the people said.

They grabbed hold of him. They said to him, "You will be put on the cross, and in retribution you will have to eat cooked pumpkin."

He tried to say that there had been a mistake, that he, not the other man, was the preacher sent by God. No one believed it. They arrived at the church. The cooked pumpkin, overdone like_bread soup, was ready, with boiling oil inside.

"Eat."

"Eat."

He ate. He was forced to. With special rope made of agave fibers joined with string, they bound him to a cross made of olive wood. It was the custom on Holy Thursday. He was not used to eating pumpkin. He suffered. He felt his stomach wrenching.

Anyway. Let's leave him, who has to play the part of poor Christ on the cross, and go to the Saracen peasant, who was in the pulpit repeating in his own fashion whatever the hidden priest suggested to him.

"Make the sign of the Holy Cross."

And the Saracen: "Don't make the sign of the Holy Cross."

The foolish people: "Whatever is he saying?"

The priest: "What are you saying, you beast?"

The Saracen: "What are you saying down there, you beasts?"

The priest was getting angry. He had the devil in his eyes: "Pig, what are you saying?"

The Saracen: "Pigs, what are you saying?"

"You're getting everything wrong. Maybe you are looking at the women's asses."

"You're getting everything wrong: are you looking at the women's asses?"

Oh, what beautiful asses some of those women had!

While the priest and the fake Discalced Capuchin preacher were talking in this way, the monk on the cross, feeling his stomach stirred as though by a cruel God, said, at first singing softly, softly, as though he were reading his Missal:

> Let me down, let me down,
> for I feel my stomach swelling,
> If you don't get me down real quick,
> I'm going to shit all over the Cross!

The people didn't understand. The playful light of the day entered every part of the church. First the children, then the men, finally the women – as though stung by laughing flies that go by in delicate flight – burst out laughing. What laughter, what guffaws! What sounds in rubies and pearls issued forth from the mouths of the women! The monk, hung with cord from the cross, cried out more loudly: "Let me down, let me down! / for I feel all my stomach swelling! / If you don't get me down real quick, / I'm going to shit all over the Cross!"

The peasants were broken up with laughter, even their clothes laughed. Because the holy feast was already underway, the bells were ringing from rooftop to rooftop. The band outside in the church square blew trumpets, trombones, horns, and clarinets. They were like the songs of birds to the glory of the Lord! In church, the false monk and the true one were swearing. That's how the feast of Holy Thursday ended up, and it wasn't a fable, but a real story that rides where it will.

The Tailor's Son

Once there was a tailor who had fallen on hard times. Carnival season arrives, reawakening the ancient heart of the people. The wind hums in the quiet forest, the river is dried up, the chill fog darkens the olive trees. In the houses there are people making sweets, people putting pleats in their clothes, people joking, people cooking meat and macaroni. For the tailor – who had three sons, a tailor's dummy, a needle, and some thread – there wasn't even any bread. The oldest boy said to his father:

"Father, my father, this year we should enjoy Carnival. Everyone is eating and laughing but us."

The tailor, with a lump of tears in his throat, replied: "And how are we to do it, my son, if we have no cash, no silver, no gold?"

"I'll take care of it, you'll see."

"Be careful, my son. Don't steal because you'll go to jail, and there life is worthless. Besides, your mother is dead, and we are alone in this sorrowful world."

"Father, my father, have no fear."

So the boy heads into the dead countryside. It held no sparkle of the sun, only stones and thorn bushes. He arrives at a vast and beautiful meadow. In the middle of the meadow the oxen of Don Antonio Fragalà, Father Superior of our town, were grazing. Seeing so many oxen the boy heaved a sigh. He listened to the plaintive cries of the calves. He saw a little one, and pulled it by the horns. He hid himself in a grotto, slit the calf's throat, removed the intestines, and took just the haunches and the shoulders. He carried it away. The young cowherd wasn't there; he had gone to the fountain. The tailor's son – let's say his name was Salvatore, to the glory of Our Lord – came back to his town in the evening. There were three street lights lit. A bell was ringing. The town was in a well of darkness. He knocks at the door. His father: "Who's that at this hour?"

"It's me, my father."

He gets up out of bed, lights the oil lamp, and goes to open the door. He grew frightened.

"All this meat, my son? I told you this would end badly. Where did you get that calf?"

"In Don Fragalà's field."

"Now you'll wind up in jail. I hear the trot of the policemen's horses, the cry of the bird."

"Don't be afraid. For now, let's eat. God be thanked."

God was thanked and adored, while they sat on the ground and ate roast veal, savory onions, hard bread. The house sparkled, outside on the roof was the beautiful white star Sirius. So...

Let's leave these people to the delights of the palate, and go to that boy of Don Antonio Fragalà's, Father Superior of our village. This boy comes back from the fountain with the jug on his back and sees that the calf named Colombo is missing.

"Colombo, Colombo," he called.

The calf's mother was lowing. You could hear that her lowing was a bitter lament. The boy runs. He jumps over ditches and blackberry bushes. He sees the town on high. He arrives, and tap, tap, he knocks.

"Who is it?" says the priest Don Antonio.

"It's me, Reverend Father."

"At this hour? What's up with you?"

"What's up with me is that the calf Colombo is missing. He's been stolen."

"And you, where were you? Who was it? How could this happen?"

"I don't know anything. I'd gone to get water."

He finished. Don Antonio made the sign of the cross, and said, "I'll find this rotten devil of a thief."

The season of Lent came, and the sky was ashen. The faithful Catholics heard the bell ringing like a river.

"Let's go to confession," they said.

The tailor was a devout Catholic, an enemy of the God Macone. He said to his son: "Salvatore, you must go to confession."

"Yes, father."

"And what will you do? What will you say to Father Superior Don Antonio?"

"I'll take care of it."

He left by the street where the rain was lightest. It was raining as fine as ash. The priest said to him: "Kneel down and tell me everything, even if you've stolen. Otherwise I can't give you the most holy consecrated Host."

In the church of Santa Maria, the peasants were on their knees on the cold marble. Some were crying here and some there, for sins committed and for the penance to be completed in beating of breasts and in the reciting of lengthy Our Fathers.

When Father Antonio Fragalà learned the facts from the young son of the tailor, he said to him, "Salvatore, here's what we'll do: there are two pulpits in the church. I'll go to one and you climb up into the other. From there you must tell the people that you stole my calf. That way all the people will be listening."

Salvatore, his head bowed, answered: "Yes sir, Father Superior."

When the boy found himself in the pulpit, he didn't say anything. He just asked Don Antonio, in a loud voice, "But do I have to say it? Do I really have to say it?" The echo of his voice grew louder over the flaming candelabras, over the jasper columns, over the heads of the peasants and of the women. The priest replied in a thundering voice: "Say it, say it! What are you waiting for, boy?"

"All right, I'll say it."

"Yes, yes, yes, so the people can hear."

"O friends, Catholic people, as you hear, it is he who is making me say it, Don Antonio, our Father Superior."

"We're listening, Salvatore," said the women.

"He's making me say that all the women here are Don Fragalà's whores."

O dark horror! The peasants ran to get hoes, mattocks, and

pitchforks. Their wives climbed up into the pulpit. The priest was impaled. His voice was a dull murmur in his throat.

"At him, at him!" said the other people who had lumbered up. There were Saracens and Frenchmen, Spaniards and Normans.

"At him, at him!"

The villagers pierced every hole in the body of Don Antonio Fragalà, who sent forth sulfurous flames from his hands and his head. This is how the fable ends. Amen, as the Lord Our Savior wished. What more do we want?

The Animals

A farmer and his wife had a donkey, and they were always in the fields in search of sun and rocks. They had a piece of land where they grew everything: string beans, broad beans, shining wheat, chick peas, blue-green lettuce, and prickly pears. All beside the little house with yellow flowers.

Now one day there was a festival in the village. Down in the valley, the farmer and his wife could see the lights in the windows, in the balconies, and on the towers where the doves sleep. The farmer's wife, sighing, said to her husband,

"Matassàro, shall we go to the village? I haven't been for seven years. That way we can see the festival."

"All right, let's go tomorrow. We need a bit of distraction."

"I'm going to wear my muslin dress. You put on your tricot pants, your blue jacket, your cap on your head, your hemp shirt, and a scarf at your neck."

Her husband replied, "What else are you going to wear?"

"My muslin skirt, my slip of light cloth, my apron, and a kerchief on my head."

The poor farmer's wife was so happy that she could hear the singing of her heartstrings. As the sun, setting beyond the dark mountain, was leaving the olive trees and the dry grass, she went on:

"Listen, Matassàro, let's take our animals with us and let's do this: Let's put some red braid on the wings of the rooster, a little purple cap on the hen, and a green ribbon on the pig's tail. We'll tint the goat's horns a beautiful color. We'll paint the turkey's beak the color of gold. We'll tie some splendid herbs in the turkey-hen's feathers."

She didn't mention the donkey. She forgot all about that poor animal sleeping all alone outside under the full moon.

The next day, as the bells were ringing from the fortress, hammering against the little streets, the roofs, the king's horse, and the houses, Matassàro went to the stall to lead out the donkey and harness it for their trip. The donkey kicked and wouldn't budge from the trough.

"Oh," he said to his wife, "the donkey doesn't want to come out. You try, Turidda."

So Turidda came with her hand raised fiercely.

"Taraccà, tarraccà, sciaccà, sciaccà," she shouted at the stubborn donkey.

All the animals were ready, gaily dressed in shimmering colors:

the cock with his shining red braid,
the hen with her purple cap,
the pig with the green ribbon,
the goat with her horns tinted green,
the turkey with his golden beak,
the turkey-hen aflower with splendid herbs.

Turidda, with ribbons in her hair, thought, "Maybe the donkey's feelings are hurt because we didn't dress him up."

So she put a cord with bells on the harness, a beautiful ribbon on his tail, and silk slippers on his hoofed feet. The donkey was so happy he brayed, and his braying made the almond tree tremble, made the circling crow shiver, made the sparrow in the roof gutters flap his wings. They went off. The village was already celebrating – people, bands, balconies wide open with tapestries of the sacred image of the Lord Our God. The bell towers, the earth, and the sky were in splendor.

"How beautiful our village looks!" said the woman. "It's like a painted lady at a balcony."

They passed through the wide square and everyone there stood and laughed at the donkey, the pig, the cock, the hen, the goat shining with braid and ribbons. Oh, how they laughed.

The farmer Matassàro said to his wife, "Let's go back to the country. These people are laughing at us."

The woman grew sad. She cried so softly. The tears flowed, and she said, "It's my fault; I was the one who said we should bring all the animals."

In the meantime, the animals, true to their nature, finding themselves the object of admiration of brides and babies, spoke up in their own fashion. They were all in harmony. The town square resounded with the sound, the very stones began to vibrate.

The cock sang "cockadoodledoo," the duck "quack, quack," the pig "oink, oink," the hen "cluck, cluck," the cardinal "chirp, chirp," the donkey "hee-haw, hee-haw."

All the animals, you know, have their own language, and if one goes "cockadoodledoo" the other answers "cockadoodledoo." In the village, from one street to another, there was a solemn assembly, just as St. Agrippina, in a white figure shining with jewels, was about to be led out of Church. The cocks pierced the air with their "cockadoodledoo," the hens with their "cluck, cluck," the ducks with their "quack, quack, quack," the pigs grunted, and the donkeys lit up the sky with long, long braying. Everyone felt happy. No one thought of sorrow, no one thought of sin, no one talked of pilgrimages to the saint's tomb, no one thought of eternity.

When Don Michele, the Father Superior, and the one hundred lesser priests that came every year from all the moonless villages heard those noises, those shouts, those whisperings, those sounds rending and plaintive or indolent from an ancient hunger, a change came over their faces.

"Oh, what's going on here? Where is this bad news coming from, that's ruining a festival that's been planned and fretted over for a year?"

Since children are like mirrors that reflect the sun, the dawn, and the noonday, they imitated the animals, and little Joey went "cockadoodledoo," little Tony went "cluck, cluck," another little one went "cheep, cheep," and little Rosina, in a little pink dress, went "cluck, cluck," and little Ciccio, Pepi, Turi, and Carmela went "uuuuu": one hell of a party!

The Father Superior, Don Michele, prayed to St. Agrippina and to the Angel Gabriel, and the lesser priests, all in black, raised their hands to the heavens.

The bell-ringers, thinking that the festival was at its height, let loose with bells that rang high and low in sounds as tiny as millet-seed, in peals as big as rocks, in trumpet blasts as high as flames and ding-dong-ding, ding-dong-ding-dong-ding, the sky, still sleepy from the recent dawn, shook with sounds that were hurled over the caps of the villagers, over the houses, over the dry stubble of the fields and valleys. The eyes of the Father Superior were slits, the hands of the lesser priests were red, the townspeople and the country folk laughed openly and out loud. The festival moved on, and here we are, barefoot and, like the moon, beaming with laughter.

Jesus Becomes a Mouse

Once upon a time an old woman craved some milk so badly that her heart was in her throat. She was standing sadly at the window when she saw some she-goats going by, laden with harness bells jingling in the shining morning air.

"O good goatherd," she said. "Will you give me a quarter liter of beautiful milk?"

He gave it to her. It frothed white in the bowl. The old woman Mary Magdalene put it in a drawer to keep it clean and flavorful. Meanwhile, the bell for Mass was heard, the roofs were still. She gets dressed and goes to church. There on the high altar in a basket of jonquils, anemones, and lilies, the Baby Jesus was sleeping. But King Frederick had heard about it, and with a stately formation of counts and barons and well-armed soldiers, he was looking for him. Someone said to the King:

"Are you looking for the little Baby? He is sleeping happily in church."

"O traitorous priest!" said the King. "And we've been looking for him through meadows and mountains."

The church was surrounded. The bell rang softly. The priest, who was a little priest with a dark cassock but a clear mind, said to Jesus: "Run away, my child! Otherwise there's no escape."

To create confusion, He, in the brilliance of his mind, said: "O my father God Macone, son of Allah, turn me into a mouse." And a mouse he became, with a silver tail and cunning eyes.

"A mouse, a mouse!" screamed the people who were on their knees praying to God, to the Goddess, to Dawn who changes Time. Imagine what happened, how the search for Jesus turned out.

"Master, everyone is escaping," shouted the soldiers. "The kingdom and the people are in terror."

Jesus was not found. The basket with jonquils was left on the altar. The little mouse Jesus went off to hide in the house of Mary Magdalene. Because he was hungry, he drank up the milk in the drawer, where he went back to sleep. She comes back, opens the drawer, and sees the empty bowl with a sleeping mouse inside. O poor wretch! She catches it. With a fierce face she snatches off his tail. Jesus-mouse wakes up from the great pain, greenish blood oozing from his missing tail. He runs away through the house, and she chases him from the table to the chair, from the chair to the night stand, from the night stand to the bed, from the bed to the nearby window illumined by the day, from the window to the roof. But he could go no further. Jesus, who felt like a mouse, was crying without his tail. He said:

"Old lady Mary Magdalene, will you give me my tail?"

She had no way of knowing that the mouse was Jesus. She had suffered too much hunger.

"I will give it to you if you bring me some milk," she relented.

The mouse goes off. He gets down off the roof. He reaches the meadow, and sees a little sheep who, tired, was napping.

He said: "Will you give me a little milk?"

"Yes, if you bring me some grass."

The mouse walked from meadow to meadow, dry from the fierce heat of the sun. He said to a garden that was dozing amidst the stones: "Garden, will you give me some grass, so I can give it to the sheep who will give me some milk? Then I will bring the milk to the old woman Mary, who will give me back my tail."

Let's turn to the garden, that said: "And how can I? Don't you see that I am sleeping on hard stones? I am so very thirsty for water."

The mouse goes off again. He crosses the shadow of an olive tree. He crosses a knoll and passes under an oak grove, knotty with thorns. He arrives at a fountain.

"O fountain, o little fountain, will you give me some water, so I can take it to the garden? That will make the grass grow, then I can bring the grass to the sheep who will give me some milk."

The fountain answered sadly: "And how can I give it to you if the cloud does not give me rain?"

The mouse had no peace. He ran through the dry woods, through the meadows without grass. He reached the tranquil sea. Jesus begged and prayed: "Oh, will you make a cloud rise up from your depths? That way you will give me rain, which I will bring to the fountain so it will give me water. The water I will bring to the garden so that it will flourish and turn green, and then give me grass that I will bring to the sheep who will make me some milk for the cruel Mary Magdalene who cut off my tail."

The sea really wanted to sleep. It unfurled some small waves that stirred very slowly. The garden of the sea lay frail and sleepy.

"You had to come along just now, o mouse?"

"But I am The Baby Jesus."

"Really? Is that true?"

Anyway, the sea felt a pang. It stirred from its depths to its surface. A very fine vapor rose up – only the eye of the dolphin saw it. A cloud was formed that, at first, with little desire for rain, went rocking and sparkling through the sky.

The mouse Jesus begged. The cloud looked down on the beach where the sea was rolling with waves.

"I beg of you, cloud, little cloud, vapor, rain cloud: I am without a tail."

The cloud, yawning again and again, said to itself: "Oh, alright." And with an affectionate caress, where the cloud flakes were all twisted up like an ear, it made the rain. The rain fell. The mouse caught it in a pitcher. He carried it to the garden where the grass sprouted on the languishing rocks.

Jesus the mouse: "O garden, will you give me some grass?"

The garden gave him some grass. He carried it to the sheep. She turned it into milk, and she felt beautiful. The mouse took the milk, and with quick steps carried it to the old woman who set aside her bitter thoughts and felt like a fresh rose. Jesus the mouse, the little mouse, got his tail back. He took it, full speed, to the ironmonger in our village, Mario Musso.

"Will you put my tail back on me? I made the old woman give

it back, for she cut it off because I drank her milk."

"OK, but you must not bite my cat, who warms me in the winter with her red eyes."

"OK, I won't bite her."

Now let's go to the ironmonger who heats up an iron rod. It rang, it sparked. He put the tail back on. The mouse said to him: "Thank you, my friend. I am Jesus who became a mouse." Don Mario Musso laughed, he said: "Jesus? I seem to have heard that name."

The mouse went away, but he fell sick. The doctor came, with his hat and the book under his arm. He examined him. He prescribed ointment of Magdalene.

"It is fragrant, and it does not sting. It calms the fever."

He put some ointment on him, but the mouse died. The mouse, our most high all-powerful Jesus, died. The bells pealed, the old woman felt forlorn and bereft. Jesus the dead mouse lay in a grotto to which all the animals of the world came: the sparrow, the sheep, the she-goat, the cock, the chick, the quivering grass, our holy bean, the cricket, the cloud itself, the exceedingly great splendor of the sun.

It is a little fable. It ends here.

Jesus' Brother

Once upon a time there was a husband and wife. They had an eight-year old daughter and a five-month old baby boy. On display in their shop they sold branches laden with cherries, broccoli, pumpkins, tangerines, the kind of lemons we call *lumie*, Hyblean honey, new wine, luscious tomatoes, liquorice root, figs in season, several kinds of lettuce, twine for weary women who might want to hang themselves, ropes for the animals, dried beans, string beans, trunks of pepper trees, and small cinnamon trees. But enough of this.

The wife takes sick. She says to her husband: "Antonio, I don't feel well." They call the doctor right away. He comes with a book under his arm and a silver-knobbed cane. He examined her. He said: "Your wife has a displaced heart. She won't get well."

That poor woman drank some cinnamon tea, gathered cherries from the branches in the shop, drank water created by Our Lord, but she got worse just the same. She lost color and skin. Just like the leaves, she was covered with shadows. The sun didn't cheer her. She died.

Her husband, Don Antonio, was left alone with two crying children. He said to himself: "How can I manage on my own? How?" The neighbor ladies saw him in a depressed state that everyday made his hands shake, and one of them said: "Don Antonio, would you like to marry Maria the Saracen, the mother of Jesus?"

"Is this possible?" he asked.

"Yes, it's possible. Her husband is dead, and her son is lost somewhere out in the world. She passes through the narrow streets always in tears."

"Then, just as you wish, I will do it for the sake of my two children."

That woman, named Agrippina, went to tell Maria as she was

carding wool. Below in the field a man with a hoe was digging out weeds that sucked up what little shining water there was for the beans.

She says: "Maria, cousin and mother of Our Jesus, we want you to get married. Can you stay always sad and by yourself? We want to give you in marriage to Master Antonio. He is well off. He has a shop full of pepper, almonds, perfumed oils, but he has two forlorn children. Do you want to marry him?"

Maria thought and said, perhaps speaking to the Angel Michael Gabriel who was as still as a rose on the King's veranda: "Is this what you wish? Is it destiny? So be it."

Amen. So it was.

Master Antonio was exceedingly happy. In the street they drank a wine like liquid crystal. That poor thing, Maria of Jesus, truly loved the two children. She treated them like a mother who gives her breasts to suck, and protects them from the dark night. This stepmother Maria then had a son, a jewel as shiny as a tiny moon. But he lived only seven months and died from illness. Oh, poor broken little silver hammer! You can imagine the father and mother. The little stepbrother, who was named Salvatore, was now seven years old. He said to his sister Pina: "Listen, let's go to the cemetery to get our brother Giovannipaolo." And they went off, innocent creatures.

That day Jesus, tired of wandering through the world which is always in pain and in war, wanted to return to his village, our very own, high on the beautiful mountain.

"Oh, how high it is!" he said to his companions Joachim and St. Francis, who never left him.

They came first to the cemetery. In those days that was where the ditch was, a cavern and deep abyss into which the poor dead were hurled. He saw among those bodies three Saracen friends with whom he had played in the streets and with whom he had flown over olive trees and roofs. He said:

"Abdullah, Camùti, Imru, wake up from your mortal sleep."

And they woke up, with frightened eyes they looked at the

world anew. Death left them, in tears it flew away.

Let's leave Jesus, happy, and go to Pina and Salvatore, who were gazing upon their dead little brother set in a little grotto inside a basket, as was the custom, full of grape vines, peaches, and flowers called lilies.

"Let's go get him, let's go get him," said Salvatore.

Pina Agrippina, who was older, was crying, and her crying like waves and her sobbing like thorns reached Jesus.

"Master," said St. Francis, "someone's crying."

"Who wouldn't cry here?" replied Joachim, always light-spirited.

They climbed up, they saw the brother and sister.

"Why are you crying?" asked St. Francis.

They told him everything.

"Their mother is Maria, mother of Jesus, our Lord?" St. Francis asked with great surprise.

Jesus spoke: "It's my brother? Ooh! Really?" And he thought, then: "My poor mother! She was alone in sorrow and she married Master Antonio."

He moved his hand. It flashed. He worked a miracle. His brother Giovannipaolo opened his eyes, saw the light again, and left the black water. Two such happy children.

"Ooooh," Agrippina cried out.

Their joy rang out. They put the basket with the baby on her head and returned to the village. The little one was dressed in white linen.

"Hurray, Hurray!" the people cried. "He's alive! Does Salvatore, son of Don Antonio, know how to work miracles?"

Men hurried forth, women, a shoemaker, the barber, the tailor. Mother Maria covered her tiny little boy with kisses. She never tired of caressing his living flesh. The priest learned of it. He said: "It's a sin, a great sin. Who wakes the dead from their dark sea? Our Lord Triune and One God does not wish it."

He ran to the Marshall. King Vittorio, who was quietly reading a book about knights, seated on his beautiful balcony where the hyacinth bloomed, learned of it.

"Who was it?" he asked.

Psst, psst, buzz, buzz, he was told.

"Jesus has returned. He's a strange fellow, he doesn't leave anyone in peace, not even the dead."

"O Your Highness, O King Vittorio, he has brought back to life even Camùti, Imru, and Abdullah!"

"The Saracens I condemned to death?"

"Yes Sir, Your Majesty."

"Arrest him immediately, sentence him."

The officer hurried with the mounted police through the countryside. Even the windows cried out, the world resounded! An old farmer named Omar said to Jesus: "Run, they are looking to arrest you. You have performed the greatest miracle possible!"

The police, the soldiers, with arrows and guns, had seen this Jesus who turned stones into bread in an alley where there were a hundred children without bread.

"Run away, Jesus, run away," shouted St. Francis.

His three friends, Imru, Camùti, Abdullah, brothers in the flesh, and St. Francis followed him. They hid themselves in a dark olive tree. Jesus runs. He enters the shop of a blacksmith, who was Mario Musso.

"Who are you?" he asked.

"I am Jesus, with my three friends."

"Jesus? And whoever might you be?"

"Save us, save us!"

"What have you done? Robbed? Killed? Have you borne false witness?"

"We brought a dead baby, Giovannipaolo, back to life."

The heart of this blacksmith was wreathed in kindness.

"And what shall I do?"

"Strike us like the iron, strike us!"

"O God, how can I do it?"

"You must do it."

He did it. He struck and struck again. Jesus' poor body became bloodied. His eyes turned black. His hand became thin. He was a bar of red-hot iron, poor Jesus!

"O Jesus, our brother! Are you leaving us in this abyss?" said the three Saracens.

"So be it!" said Don Mario.

Hurriedly he struck and struck again the bodies of Imru, Camùti, and Abdullah. They sent off sparks. They twisted and turned into iron, yellow with fire.

"Where is Jesus? Where are the three Saracens, his brothers and friends?" asked the police, commanded by the officer who, rough and cruel, stopped before the shop on his steaming horse.

"Who are you talking about?"

"Are you playing dumb?"

"Look and you'll see."

What was there for them to find? Bars of hot iron, still giving off sparks.

The officer grew angry: "So where have they gone, these Saracens of the devil?"

There was no Jesus under the anvil. There was no Imru under the forge. There was no Camùti under the ashes. There was no one there!

The horses, pale and wan, began again to paw the ground. Don Mario piled the bars up among the others already worked and finished. He went off home to have a dinner of beans and onions.

Next morning (when he came to get the bars for the iron gate that King Vittorio wanted to put up at Minèo to protect himself from robbers, bandits, Saracens, thieves, tricksters, jokesters, musicians, and cheaters) Don Mario couldn't tell which was Jesus, which was Camùti, which was Abdullah.

"O St. Agrippina, what shall I do?"

He thought, he said to himself: "And is it my fault if I had to deal with these madmen? Would they have been better off with the justice of our Catholic King?"

He delivered everything, even the bars in which, like buds and blossoms of heavenly iron and light, Jesus and his three brothers and friends lived. And so they became the gate of our village, the gate of Jacò, or Bacchus, as others call it.

With Jesus' disappearance, the life force of his little baby brother Giovannipaolo ended. He died again, in a flash. Poof! He was no longer like the singing cicada, but like a buried cricket. He was no longer a rooster, but a feather in the wind. He was no longer grain, but burnt stubble. His mother was in tears, no one could calm her, she would not be comforted.

The hundred priests of the village said: "The will of the Eternal is done. Whoever dies does not come back to life." The bells rang out; tears fell on the roofs. The hundred priests – some limping, some trembling, some with red cheekbones – gave orders to sing hymns and lullabies and to lower little Giovannipaolo, dressed in a linen cloth spun with silver, forever into the asphodel plain of death.

We're up here in light and on the banks, and he's down there, little nightingale, in the dark. That's the way it is.

The Parrot

After King Ased, Our Lord and Ruler, died, Giovanni Del Ridere was made head of the people, and in a short time he ruled over everyone. He ruled over the poor who lived on bread and honey. He ruled over the old woman who prayed to God morning and night. He ruled over the shoemaker who worked in his shop. He ruled over the cart driver who travels through mountains and valleys. He ruled over the engineer who guides the train over its iron rails. He ruled over the worker who labors in the chill of the morning!

Anyway. One time he saw a bird with colored wings flying low.

"Oh, how beautiful it is. Catch it!"

And the soldiers ran and caught it.

"What is it?"

"It's a parrot, Our lord, Head of the People."

He taught it to speak, first one word, then another.

"I give you the name Ciccio," Giovanni Lord Head of the People said to it. And Ciccio it was. He told his owner everything.

"Master, the shoemaker is sleeping."

"Master, the engineer is eating."

"Master, the poor people are going to Mass."

This gentleman, who was like a King and Lord, had a chambermaid named Elena, a girl of twenty-two years. Since she was very thin and wanted to put on some weight, in secret she was stealing from her master: now some meat, now some fresh mozzarella, now sugar, now cherries when they were gathered from the branching tree. The parrot told Giovanni Head of the People everything.

"Master, Elena is eating pheasant."

"Master, Elena is eating bread and honey."

"Master, Elena has gotten engaged to an engineer named

Antonio."

One day the young chambermaid said to herself: "I can't stand it anymore." She talked about it to her engineer boyfriend Antonio. "Oh, what shall I do, my darling love?"

He had a thought.

"Sew up the parrot's ass."

Now this parrot, like an evil wizard, had managed to bring all the people under its influence, even the chaste and pure who lived in solitary forests.

If the parrot said: "Beautiful," the soldier said "Beautiful." If the feathered, flying animal said: "What a grey day," the shoe-maker, the tobacconist, the postman, the Marshall, the teacher, the director, the druggist, and the grocer said: "What a grey day!"

She couldn't stand it anymore. So the girl Elena sews up the parrot's ass. She used a copper wire. The master Head of the People saw the dejected parrot. It didn't talk. It didn't preen its feathers.

"O my Ciccio, what's the matter?"

"Sewn-up ass, Master."

He didn't understand. He had too many things to do, what with the police, the laws, tribunals, and outbursts of fighting. But it troubled him.

One morning Master Giovanni Head of the People gets up early, as the dawn turns the roofs of the great city to silver, and he sees the dead parrot.

"O my Ciccio, what will I do without you?"

He called Elena.

"Do you see my dead parrot? Who did it?"

"How should I know, Master Sir Giovanni?"

"He was always saying to me 'sewn-up ass, master'."

"And how am I supposed to know anything about it?"

Giovanni thinks about it. He looks at the parrot's rear plumage, the faded blue feathers, and he sees that the flying feathered animal really did have its ass sewn up. He became furious. He called the chambermaid Elena.

"It was you! You!"

He was no longer cheerful. He wasn't happy. Evil fell over his soul. First he had an elaborate tomb made for the parrot Ciccio, amidst branches of poplars and black cypresses, and an imitation moon imprinted on a golden sky of papier-maché. And he had all the people in there to pray:

"O our parrot Ciccio!"

"O brother parrot!"

"O our Lord and Master!"

Next Giovanni King and Head of the People gave the order to sew up the ass of everyone:

> the early-rising laborer,
> the old man with the bulbous nose,
> the most dedicated director,
> the conductor who at all hours
> drives the train; the postman,
> the great and famous cook; the soldier,
> the cop who administers poison,
> the enterprising salesman!

Oh, our poor people who could no longer attend to their usual affairs!

Since there was, higher up, an almost mirror image of this hole – the mouth hole –, it was also sewn up on the merchants, citizens, country villagers – on everybody everywhere. Even the rocks cried all the time, and the rain that made no noise. The very sun cried upon seeing that men, little by little, no longer had loving passions and quiet nights, but became thin as ghosts, like specters that, in the semblance of men, were a string of bones from head to foot! An entire people disappeared: the peasant in the forest, the citizen in the house, the bather on the odorless shore, the minister, the son of King Frederick, who was languishing in a deep, dark cell. Whenever they met each other, they would ask – they were very long, thin phantasms: "Who are you?" "Where do you come from?"

"Where are you going?"

In the whole of the kingdom permeated by the prayers and laments of the people that – poof! – disappeared into the vortex of the sky, there remained only these, used to eating nothing but the air fleeing over the roofs and rosy shadows, onions, cooked beans, and little curled-up worms:

> *Turi the artichoke,*
> *Sariddu the hunchback,*
> *Ciccio the matchstick,*
> *Peppi the doorpost,*
> *Cicciu the dogpisser,*
> *Antoniu the glutton,*
> *Matteu the oil vendor,*
> *Angiuzzu the chicory vendor.*

The Little She-donkey

One time Jesus saw Sister Catherine, called "The Sienese" because she had burning eyes and a beautiful lock of black hair on her forehead and a thick veil at her white neck, and he said, "Oh, how beautiful my little she-donkey is."

And she-donkey she became, poor unfortunate child. The sisters, who numbered one hundred and one, when they saw that beast with the skinny rump, chased her away. Closed in the black convent with cypresses and pear trees along the wall, they continued to pray to God.

"Tarraccà, tarraccà, little she-donkey. You are surely the devil."

They threw a saddle cloth of fine red silk on her. An old woman who every day went to work in the country saw that she-donkey and said, "My little she-donkey, you are my good fortune." This peasant farm lady of our village had a very close friend, Signora Angelina, with whom she even shared dreams: if the one dreamed, let's say, of San Sebastiano of Melilli crying under a fig tree, the other dreamed of the sister of San Sebastiano laughing under an apricot tree.

The old woman loaded everything on the little she-donkey: faggots, stinging brambles, chicory, oregano, and jugs with water from the fountain. She returned to the village when it was dark and the night, in dark tongues, filled the whole world.

One day she said to her close friend Angelina, "You know, I have to go to Albero Bianco to take something to eat to my son who is working there amidst the wind and the rocks. Can you look after my she-donkey for me?"

"Certainly, dear friend, certainly."

And she left it in the stall. This dear friend Angelina, a kindly woman, had a very sick daughter. She said to her mother: "Listen, I have a hungering for donkey liver."

"And where am I going to find it, daughter of mine, lost in the desert of illness?"

"I know that your good friend has left you the she-donkey."

"So I should kill the she-donkey?"

"Mother mine, I have a hungering for donkey's liver. That way I could drive away this sickness that is sucking me up."

The mother cried. She was crying for her daughter and she was crying for the she-donkey that was calmly eating hay in the manger.

Out of the great affection that she had for her daughter, she took a large knife, went down into the stall, and slit the throat of the little she-donkey that turned her delicious female eyes to the distant sky. She died, oh unhappy she-donkey, Catherine of Siena of the Ursuline Nuns.

"O, my God, our Eternal Father," the woman uttered in mournful prayer. "Forgive me. Love for one's child is blind."

She takes the she-donkey, and cuts open the belly that gave off soft vapors, as though it were a meadow of roses in the morning. She takes out the liver. It wasn't a big liver, but tiny like that of a doe. It oozed blood; the internal eye of its spirit was sorrowing. She made an omelette with it, with onions that restore health, garlic that keeps away torment, basil that turns into fragrance, and fresh, tender herbs. The omelette gave off fragrant and beautiful odors, and the neighbors:

"Oh, what is this heavenly scent of paradise?"

The girl, completely happy, ate the liver. Her stomach made trumpeting noises, as if angels were closed up inside there.

Meanwhile the doctor was going from street to street, knocking at doors where a cross indicated there were sick people. He arrived, wearing a hat, and with a book under his arm. He examined the girl. He found her much better.

"And what has she eaten?" he asked.

Her mother, upset over the cruel deed, related everything.

"Oh," said the medical doctor, "she is getting better and better, but now what are you going to say to your good friend?"

"It's true. What should I do? I'm drowning in confusion."

"Bah! What do you want me to say? You'll have to see to it yourself. Let's hope that your daughter doesn't suffer ill effects from that contaminated donkey liver. It's not good to eat, you know. Well, I'm going."

And off he went. Evening came, accompanied by dark night, and the old woman returned.

"Oh, will you give me back my she-donkey?"

"The she-donkey? Wait while I come down."

Tic, tac, tic, tac, she came down the stairs. Then, "My dear friend, do you know what has happened to me?"

"What's happened to you, dear friend?"

With her eyes, her hands, in a thin voice, she related everything.

"O St. Agrippina, what have you done?"

The old woman held back her tears. Then in a fit she boiled over, she erupted.

"Either you give me the she-donkey, or you give me your beautiful daughter. Either you give me the she-donkey, or you give me your beautiful daughter."

The mother was crying, she felt the bird of night descend into her heart. Her old friend, angry as could be, went off.

A day went by, two days went by, three days went by, and enough. Her daughter was cured, but to her mother's horror, her appearance was changing. Her eyes were no longer shining and soft. Her voice was no longer singing, for even the pitch of her voice was changing. The old lady would not let up. Every evening, when the bell tower played the Ave Maria, which said with every peal that we are nothing but shadows, she would return and say: "Either you give me the she-donkey or you give me your beautiful daughter."

The daughter now had hairy ears, not white alabaster ones. She had a wrinkly forehead, no longer crystal clear. A tail had even sprung up on her, poor beautiful creature! The woman's husband said to her, "And what are we going to do with a daughter who's a donkey? It shames the neighborhood as well."

They gave her to the old woman.

"Hurray, hurray, you've bought me a new donkey!" she said.

She went off. She left the ancient circle of the village, and from the valley went up to the mountain where the sharp exterminating wind rises. But the she-donkey, who had both the heart of the Ursuline sister St. Catherine, and the heart of Ermenegilda, the daughter of her friend, had no peace. First she wanted to go into the dark woods, then towards the merry brook.

"Oh, this donkey finds no rest," said the old woman. "What shall I do? If I pull it this way, it goes that way. If I pull it that way, it goes this way. I've got an inferno on my hands."

She talked herself into letting it go. No one saw it ever again, except when there was no moon and the village was dark, pitch dark, at which time that sorrowing she-donkey would go knock with its hooves at the house of friend Angelina.

"Who is it at this hour?"

"I am your poor unfortunate daughter, mother."

She came out dressed in mourning, but she didn't see anyone.

"Who is it that is knocking at my door in the dark night?"

The she-donkey Catherine-Ermenegilda had run off in a loving trot straight to the convent.

"Who is knocking at our door at such a late hour?" asked the one hundred and one sisters who, amidst white lily flowers were praying to their God, bowing down in dance, one before the other.

"I am Sister Catherine, your unfortunate sister."

The hundred and one of them looked out. The street was dark, they saw no one. The poor she-donkey returned to her mother Angelina, crying desperately.

It is said that even now a she-donkey wanders through the fields and the forests and rivers which roll in a shining of fish, and if anyone meets up with it, they will see an animal with young skin and eyes of great beauty that sometimes weep and sometimes laugh.

She wanders back and forth, and here we sit, eating cooked fava beans and baccalá.

The Monks of the Evil Convent

A husband and wife used to beg for alms because they were poor, and poverty is a punishment, it bears no fruit. One day they met many poor people who were leading some donkeys by their halters. The husband, goodman Ciccio Casaccio, asked, "Who's selling donkeys?"

"No one."

"So where did you get them?"

"Far away on the holy mountain of Calvary there's a convent with a hundred monks, brothers, and big, fat friars."

"And so?"

"So, if you sow their fields, harvest the olive trees, and do the threshing, if with big grindstones you turn their white grain into light flour, if by night when it's dark you guard their monastery, they'll reward you with a donkey like this."

"Oh, what a lot of work you have to do!"

The wife of goodman Ciccio Casaccio the farmer said, "Ciccio, do you think you'll always be able to live off alms? Let's go."

Let's leave the husband and wife, who set out through hot passages, through dried-up paths, through the straits of rocky caverns. Enough. In the convent the hundred monks, young and old, were holding Jesus prisoner, chained up with smooth cords of gold, held rigid by rings in the walls. Since they knew he could turn stones into bread, they ordered him to turn the donkeys that Father Gaudenzio painted into real donkeys. The villagers knew of the affair, and in order to own a beast they went there to work, sweating night and day, so that those harsh lands had become like veiled gardens bedecked with gems, fields where fava beans, chick peas, grain, and barley blossomed.

Goodman Ciccio and his wife Signora Maruzzedda arrive.

"Halt!" they hear someone say. "Who are you?"

"We're looking for work."

"We can only give you a donkey."

"OK," said Ciccio the farmer.

"OK," his wife said, in an echo that died in the blond wheat.

Since it was the time of the grape harvest, the monks put gags in the mouths of the husband and wife so they wouldn't be able to taste the clusters of grapes that shone there, to the glory of God. O dark desire, o glances, o sighs! The two poor people worked those convent lands for a year, a month, and a day. They ate herbs, straw, and the occasional modest little bean.

"Here's your donkey," the Father Superior named Gaudenzio said to them.

And as they went away so skinny, with their bones sticking out, they saw the monks fat and rosy, singing a sacred hymn to God. But in a cavern they saw a young man chained up.

"Oh, my son, who are you?"

"I am Jesus. They keep me here to perform miracles."

"Always chained up?"

"Yes. If you see my friend Giufà, the giant, tell him to come and free me."

"Of course, handsome youth. O what an evil fortune is yours."

Jesus, seeing that their hearts were softened like fading light, knew that they were good people, and so he said, "I will put a charm on your donkey."

In the countryside there were many donkeys, but they were badly nourished with barren hay, and they were dying. They whitened the meadows and fields with bones, and they blackened them with dead black donkeys.

"Let's get out of here, my husband. Where there's a monk, there's hell. Thank God they've given us this old donkey."

On the other side, towards the faraway village, the earth shed tears. You could see blazing valleys, barren summits.

They arrived home when the bell of evening was ringing. The bell rang as far as the eye can see. Once they got home, the stall was scarcely large enough for Ciccio the farmer and his wife. The husband said, "The donkey will sleep at our feet. We've got hay."

The poor neighbors peered in at windows so small their heads wouldn't fit. "Oh," they said, "what an ugly, skinny, dying donkey! Where did you find it?"

"You know the old saying?" said goodman Ciccio the farmer angrily. "It goes: 'Don't interfere in other people's business; don't get mixed up in other people's affairs, for no good deed goes unpunished'."

The people went off. It was time to sleep, the full pealing of the bell said so. The cocks were already sleeping. The hen was asleep. The crows were in their rocky holes, the crane in its nest. The eagle was dreaming. The nightingales were asleep, along with the sparrow, the thrushes, and the missel thrushes.

"Oh, what bad luck," his lady wife was saying. "How much will it cost us to feed this donkey? And what use can he be to us?"

And then what happened? During the night, the donkey all of the sudden farted so loud that it shook the dark house. The wife shouted, "The donkey has shit out everything, Ciccio."

"Quiet! Light the lamp."

It was a pale light, a red cross. Ciccio the farmer gets out of bed and sees that the donkey has shit ever so many gold pieces. They were still wriggling on the stones of the stall.

"Oh, oh! O wife, little wife, dear wife, a fortune, a real fortune!"

In the meantime the donkey farted again. This time the money landed all warm in the face of Ciccio the farmer, shining in his mouth. How many of them he shat out!

"How you sparkle, Ciccio!"

His wife, seeing what happened, started to dance for joy, hearing her husband shout, "We're rich, and nobody knows it but us! We're rich, and nobody knows it but us!"

Our holy earth turned in the sky like a woman in an apron, happy as can be. The stars watched her. The woods danced along with the bird, the river, and the mountain. Her husband shouted, "We're rich! Now we'll buy ourselves the castle of Prince Pupù!"

Into that joy of the world came the day, with the song of the cock and the cluck of the hen. Ciccio and his wife opened the door, and there in the alley were people, poor people. Even the dogs had come. Everybody knew about it. The children cried, in sweet lament, "And you're not going to give us anything?" The woman, with one bare foot, "Are you the only ones who are children of our Omnipotent God?" The old people, "So maybe we don't have eyes?"

Goodman Ciccio spoke: "Wife, my dear little wife, here everyone is looking at us with their own kind of reason: logical reason, metaphysical reason, and contemplative reason."

"We don't have to give away anything, Ciccio! We're poor. Everyone thinks of his own poverty."

But the donkey shit gold pieces in continuation — what was it, a river? The children came, the women came, the villagers came. Even counts and princes came. They filled up sieves, baskets, chests, bowls, and caps. Even the sparrows stole gold pieces to make beautiful nests. Into those parts came Orlando, the great knight. He was tired, all night long he had been pursuing Angelica.

"O our Orlando, O our dear Orlando," shouted the men. "Take some gold pieces."

He filled his helmet. Then he said, modestly, "Enough, brothers. Where the need is greater, lesser need gives way."

In honesty and kindness he went off into a sun that happily followed him with its long tail through woods and solitary valleys.

They, happy and content, and we, barefoot and without a thing.

Fables

The White Girl Named Maria

Once there was a girl named Maria, daughter of Joachim, who was born of Giovanni, son of Salvatore, who was the son of Michael Gabriel, born of Mulìd. One day, her father and her mother Anna said to their daughter: "Would you like to go to the Lake of the Dead Sea?" The Lake of the Dead Sea stretched over a dry land, with neither trees nor the call of a flying swallow. That's what they say. The daughter said yes. Afterwards, in secret, the mother said to the father, "I'm afraid, Joachim, that the fishermen might fall in love with our daughter's great beauty." In fact, Maria was like crystal, lovely and graceful, with crimson lips which, whenever she spoke, brought forth fragrant flowers.

They set off. There was no road. Walking through those barren plains were animals called camels. The sun was aflame, even the little sand gods wriggled away to escape. As soon as they came to the quiet waves of that clear lake, some of the fishermen began gazing at that girl called Maria.

"Oh, how beautiful she is!" they said among themselves. "Like a verdant field."

An old man, hooded against the burning sun, asked her in a loud voice from the opposite shore, "Who are you? What's your name?"

"They call me Maria."

"O Maria, beautiful flesh of Our God."

As the girl Maria, beautiful and white, was speaking, flowers of yellow, green, and red issued forth from her mouth. The girl, seeing that the fishermen kept looking at her with desire in their eyes and hands, said shyly to her mother, "Mother Anna, let's go." She answered, "You have beautiful lips and a divine forehead, my daughter. I told your father they would devour you with their gazes."

Her father said, "There is an inlet of water over there. Don't you at least want to take a dip in the waves and cool yourself off?"

"No, no one should see my flesh."

They went back through those yellow lands, and when they were close to town, out came the King, the knights with cuirass and sword, the Prince with shining eyes. He saw Maria and said to his father, from his dark horse with its black hooves:

"King Herod, my father, who is that?"

The King gave orders to stop the carriage with its four neighing horses, drawing near the rocks of the desert.

Oh, what a grip! Oh, what a carriage! The King got down, his black beard darkened his chin.

"Get in, my ladies, we will escort you."

The girl was frightened. She was exceedingly beautiful, with her golden strands of blond hair. The Prince, seeing her, with flowers and blossoms in her mouth when she talked, fell deeply in love. But Maria knew that King Herod had a dark nature. Her mother Anna said to her: "My daughter, you must get in. You can't say 'no' to our sovereign." They escorted them to the borders of the land of the Pharisees that was even more barren, without fragrant sprouts or leafy trees. The Prince, during that trip, said to his father, "I am in love with Maria." The King replied, "Do you want to marry her?" "Yes, father." He didn't reply, but the Prince's mother said to Maria, as she got down, "My son, the Prince of the Judaic people, is in love with you." Maria fashioned a reply: "I will marry when I've finished weaving a cloth." The Prince answered, with golden bells in his heart: "Yes, I will marry you. I will wait."

So... They bade each other farewell. They went off, Maria with her mother, Anna, and her father, Joachim.

Three years, a month, and a day went by, and Maria sent no further news of herself to the Prince, who, prompted by his father, thought that the girl had woven him a trap. One day the Prince said to his mother:

"I have had no news from that girl, no word."

"Why not, my son?" His mother summoned a lady-in-waiting

and said to her, "Mafalda, you must go to the house of that girl." She answered, "The girl lives far away, on the mountain where the sun rises."

The Prince immediately calls for his coachman and orders him to make ready a carriage with two horses, one black and one white as milk. "Accompany Mafalda." "Yes, Your Majesty Prince Jehosaphat."

The coachman travels with the lady through grey roads, through lands without green trees. The immense countryside was pierced by the sun. They went up a small hill and down into a plain. They went through a wood of dry olive trees. Again they went up the hill to reach the mountain, while black birds flew all around them.

They arrived at a simple house with a thatch roof and yellow clay walls.

"I wish to speak with your daughter," said the lady of the court.

"With my daughter?"

"King Herod has sent me."

"O God, Our Savior."

"Don't be afraid. I'm here because of that promise."

Maria appeared, beautiful, blonde, with her hair all golden strands. Mafalda, the lady-in-waiting, fell in love with her. Her flesh was too beautiful, too fine, this Maria. And then, those flowers and blossoms that came forth from her mouth when she spoke!

"Prince Jehosaphat sent me. He wants me to ask you 'How did it turn out?'. He's waiting to marry you."

"Signorina, lady-in-waiting, I am not going to marry anyone."

Having bid her farewell, the lady Mafalda went off through the trails and paths in the eye of the dying sun. The Prince was watching from his terrace. Through his silver telescope, the entire countryside was lit up. He said to himself, "They are arriving." Immediately, Prince Jehosaphat goes down and questions the lady as she is about to descend from the carriage, dimmed by the evening shadows:

"So, how did it turn out?"

"It turned out, Sir Prince, that she does not desire marriage."

The Prince became frightened, his soul and his wrists trembled.

King Herod learned of it. A bloodthirsty man, ready to deal out death, and with his eyes full of poison, he called for the executioner to kill Maria, daughter of Joachim and Anna. When the extinguished light returned to the world, the soldiers with helmets and swords along with the executioner left for the mountain. The Prince, learning of the matter, cried. The Queen Mother cried; Mafalda and all the people of the Judaic realm cried. And so...

The girl Maria was seized.

"The order of our King is that you must be killed."

Her mother Anna was frightened. She dropped her head into her hands. The white beard of her vulnerable father trembled. The soldiers, whom did they take away? Maria. The father and mother of the girl also went, treading the reddened roads without a blade of glass. The Prince, in sorrow, went out from his magnificent house to see Maria executed. With his band of knights, he passed through a woods where the birds sang ceremoniously. The Prince had informed Maria, "If you marry me, I will save you from a violent death." She, completely calm, with jeweled buds in her mouth, said, "I will not marry. No one should behold my flesh."

Already the trumpets were sounding. It was the order for death. They were sounding in sorrow. In the nearby woods the birds sang no more.

The scaffold was readied. People gathered to watch (some were happy because they were hostile to religion, and some had hearts of darkness). Maria, daughter of Joachim, mounted the scaffold, for they were to cut off her head. The executioner cast a very long shadow.

So. Just as the Prince, violating the orders of his father the King, was saying, "Stop, stop, don't touch her," all of the sudden Anna disappeared, Joachim disappeared, no longer was Maria there, but a quivering white river in the heavens. A strip embroidered in gold remained, which read, "I am St. Anna, my husband is Joachim, my daughter is Maria, mother of Jesus."

Everyone was frightened, realizing that Maria was the mother of Jesus. The knights remained with their swords aloft. The executioner fell dead upon the scaffold. The faithful, lay people and religious, went out, dispersed through dark caves, into the world.

They say that King Herod was enraged. He gave orders to kill all the beautiful children.

It's a story, you know, without cries and lamentations, but with flowers and blossoms in the mouths of the good girls.

Lady Catherine

A lady of high birth, with a most beautiful figure, had a lady companion named Maria. This lady, named Catherine, had given herself over to worldly life. She delighted in pleasures, in guitars and songs, and she fed on men. She lived in a palace on a high, angry mountain, where clouds and stormy rains arose. And so...

Catherine would say to that good, innocent Maria: "Listen, you must keep watch from the balcony, and if you see a wandering knight, call to him."

She leans out. She waits, and at last she sees a young knight coming through the weeds and new grass, with his trusty sword at his side. She calls to him, "Listen, young man, my Lady wishes to speak with you."

He went up the great staircase, with statues that bowed down at his passing. He arrived at the top. He asked: "May I come in?"

The horse stamped in the courtyard, his mane like a frightful wind.

Catherine replied, "Come in, come in." And he: "Good day, My Lady." "How do you have the courage, handsome youth, to cross the kingdom of King Herod on your own?"

"It is my destiny to travel through deserts and rocks."

They began to talk. Catherine dared not look at him. Then, feeling fire in her hands, fire in her face, fire in her legs, she embraced him and kissed him all over. She said to him, "Do you wish to stay with me this evening?" The young knight, whose helmet shined in the dying sun, answered, "With great pleasure." Catherine calls Maria, also young but with the bloom now gone from her face. She said to her: "Listen, prepare a sumptuous dinner. This evening don't come to my room." "All right, I understand, my Lady of Siena." Catherine embraced her. She said to her: "Maria, what a beautiful name you have. Full of lilies and roses."

When the meal was ready, Catherine entered the room where the youth was waiting for her and she said, "Shall we dine?" He answered, "As you wish, my Lady."

Immediately the table was laden with pheasant on a spit, ricotta, honey, cooked fava beans, bread, all manner of things. They ate, and the sun left those desolate lands still shining in the Judaic desert, going down, down, through the arms of the valleys and the dead sea.

Catherine said to him, "Let's go to bed after the meal, as is the custom among the knights of old." The bed was all in flower. All around were green plants. They looked at each other with eyes of love, and they spent the night in play and laughter. When it was day, with the sun that rose up from the mountains, the young man, his mind fresh, put on his cuirass and sword. He bade her farewell and went away. The horse's hooves could be heard on the white basalt.

Catherine of Siena led this life for more than four years. One time there came to her the painter Ciotto, quite famous throughout the district and the valleys. He ate. He lay with my Lady Signora Catherine, and in tribute he painted on the walls of the staircase the distant Pope, blond Sir Frederick, and the light of the moon. But enough of this.

One day, while Maria was gazing at the valley, she saw a most handsome young man who, with black hair and precious eyes, was making his way through the world alone.

"There's a really handsome young man," said Maria.

"Call him, call him."

"O beautiful lost youth, my Lady wants you."

She runs to meet him. She kisses him all over. He had sad and precious eyes. From every part of his body there issued so much blood. Catherine took him by the hand. She asked him, "What is it, knight? Are you wounded?" The young man said, "I am neither wounded nor hurt, and I do not want help, not even from

Catherine."

"Well, then, let's go to the table to eat, as is the custom among knights of old." Catherine herself sets the table — pheasant, honeyed fava beans, and sweets — but the youth did not eat. Catherine cuts the bread. She gives it to him, but the bread sheds blood. Catherine asks, "So, who are you?"

"I am the Prince of the World."

"Greater than our King Herod?"

"My kingdom has no end."

"But are you wounded?"

"I am neither wounded nor hurt, and I do not want help, not even from Catherine."

"Well, then, let's go to bed, as is the custom among knights of old."

They go up the stairs, where the pictures of every color by the painter Ciotto glimmer in beauty.

> And when the Prince ascended the stairs
> he washed the stairs in blood.
> And when the Prince sat in a chair
> he washed the chair in blood.

Catherine removes the covers, smelling of lilies and powder. She turns but she sees the beautiful youth no longer. On the bed was stamped the sad figure with the precious eyes of Jesus. From faraway a voice said, in a sigh of love, "Come tomorrow to my castle."

Catherine began to scream. Maria hurries to her and finds she has fainted, beautiful as a bouquet of violets. When Catherine comes to, she says, "Maria, tomorrow we must go to the Castle of Paradise." Maria looked at the bed. She sees the sad image of Jesus.

"O God, O my God," she screamed.

"Why are you screaming?" asked Catherine.

"O God, O God. That is Jesus, my son, who was lost in the

world of our desert."

Catherine grows frightened. She says, "You are Maria, the mother of Jesus?" They cried. They went to bed. That night the sun stayed on the mountains and forests. It did not set.

Rested, Catherine calls the coachman. He came with the carriage that was white with shining gold trim. The coachman, reining in the four horses, said: "My Lady, where are we off to?"

"To the Castle of Paradise, in Trieste."

They left. The valley was filled with the sounding horn and sparkling hooves. When they arrived, they found the gate with a golden key. They unlocked it. Catherine opens the gate. She finds a staircase all covered with carpets, and on the sides, vases with blue flowers. She climbs up and finds the rooms done in green, blue, and rose velvet. Four rooms were all in gold, and Catherine gazed around her, stunned. One picture showed the Baby Jesus in the desert amidst merchants with bristly beards. He was speaking.

Catherine was frightened by the beauty she found. The coachman was frightened by all that glittering gold. Catherine remained a long time in the castle. She asked pardon of Jesus. She ate only bread and water for penance. But every two days, a cow who understood the speech of humans came up to Catherine, and offered her full teats. My Lady Catherine of Siena filled a jug with milk.

Catherine was in perpetual penance, and when she remembered those many young lovers she fell into a deep depression. This grew worse. It was like a wound which bore into her flesh.

Maria, who was the mother of Jesus, was now beautifully dressed, with a silk shawl and sapphire stones on her shoes. One day Catherine said to her, "Maria, I don't feel well." "Let's go into the garden to get some air." There were fig trees, almond trees, olive trees, carob trees, azarole trees, mulberry trees, and apricot trees.

Catherine sat down. She thought she saw in a vision young men on horseback whose horses were pawing at the reddish soil.

The two women were seated on a bench painted in the finest and most subtle of colors. Then a white dove fluttered down, with a golden crown on its head. Catherine said, "Catch it." Maria said, "I can't catch it." The fluttering bird perched on Catherine's shoulders. It left behind the crown and flew back to its celestial dwelling in the heavens. Catherine said again to Maria, "Let's go in the house, I don't feel well." They slowly, slowly, climbed the stairs. Catherine got into bed. She entered into agony. She was thirty-three years old. An angel came, with a crown of shining gemstones. To Catherine in agony it seemed to be a knight with a rich mantle. (O unhappy lover!)

The angel left the body of Lady Catherine of Siena. It carried her soul, in a splendor of copper and silver, away into Paradise. On earth, the Judaic desert closed itself up in shadows.

The story is told, the story is written; tell me yours, for mine is done. Catherine in heaven, to her good fortune, and we here in our dark village.

The Little Green Horse

A farmer had four pieces of land in a field so desolate that it was touched only by the rays of the sun. He had four daughters, and the most beautiful was Tamàr. On their way to work in the field, they passed through a small lane full of dazzling light. The olive trees that could be seen here and there looked sad and forsaken. As the girls were clearing the grain of weeds and violet-colored cornflowers, a trot was heard in the distance that jolted the grain and whirled in the sheaves of wheat.

"Could it be the knight-errant Orlando?" wondered the father, Taddeo Caldeo the farmer.

"Can he be passing this way?" asked the oldest daughter, her eyes gazing out into the blond wheat.

Instead, up rose a little green horse. It was a colt with a thousand spirits in each hoof. In its passing this little horse trod upon all the grain.

"Tarraccà, tarraccà," said the four daughters, beating the air with their hands. Their father, the farmer Taddeo, was very angry about that little horse. The girls said: "If it comes back again, we'll kill it."

That evening they returned to their house, passing along a slope and then through a steep rise that was covered by the endless shadow of evening. In the morning they got up and went out to reap the grain good and clean. In the town one cock crowed, two cocks crowed, three cocks crowed.

The girls arrive in the field with their father Taddeo Caldeo. A loud, loud noise is heard. The ripe grain bowed its head. Golden darts shot out from the eyes of the little horse, and its hooves made whistling sounds. It passed through the field, trampling the sheaves. It went without caution: it was wolf and lion and fleeing child. "Tarraccà, tarraccà," shouted the girls. As little Tamàr ran in pursuit, the wind opened up before her in obedience.

She came to a palace set on a dark, hostile mountain. She saw the little horse enter the castle. The girl goes in. She hears many voices speaking, and heard, without seeing anyone: "Come, come, beautiful Tamàr, for here lives the god of the moon; under enchantment, he has been turned into a horse." The girl felt her little feet grow weak with fear.

She gathered courage. She went forward, the voices always calling her, now very faint, and Tamàr replied, her words had a reed-like sound: "My name is Tamàr. Who are you?" But she didn't see anyone. She couldn't see anyone in that castle of mystery.

In the evening the countryside grew dim as it turned from light to dark. The girl named Tamàr bedded down in a room full of luxurious things. The silence made her face turn pale. So...

Midnight came. The silence was getting thicker and a sound like thunder was heard. The castle danced with the sound. Tamàr was afraid. In a great white light the little green horse appeared. It shook its ears, its back, its tail. A light ran over its body. It turned into a handsome young man. He looked as fresh as new grass.

He ascends the staircase. Seeing the girl, he grew frightened and asked: "And who are you?" The poor thing, she told him everything, and he said: "Was it I who trampled the ripe blond grain? But if I did not do so, the earth would not regenerate: my shining hooves cause it to be reborn."

"Who are you?"

"I am the god of the moon that passes through the sky."

"And how can you be freed?"

"You have to catch the four horses that are the horses of the sun, who has me imprisoned in this green darkness. If I am not freed, the moon will always remain in the depths."

All of the sudden he disappeared, but his spirit remained in the air like a white lily. Tamàr at first was confused, then she spoke some words to the mysterious voices of the dark castle: "O voices, my friends, forces that cause the wandering moon to rise in the sky, I would like a favor from all of you. I want the four horses, all bound in white chains, so I can free the young lunar God."

And they said: "If you're going to free our son the Prince, free us too, for we are souls damned in this dark inferno." And all around a noise was heard, like the disturbing cry of the dead.

This passed. At midnight the little green horse arrived. The four horses were already in chains. The little horse, as soon as he appeared, gave off the usual sudden light, like sparks. The four horses broke their chains. The castle crumbled with a sigh, and disappeared. The little horse turned back into a beautiful handsome god. He embraced Tamàr, then he said: "You know, we must go to my kingdom." They walked through the desert where only little red flowers were seen in the rocks. They came to what looked like a large ravine. It was evening. The people in the villages walked in procession within the quiet dream. Our Lord prince the little green horse said to Tamàr: "Let us go down into the depths."

"Oh, where are you taking me?"

"To my splendid kingdom."

Not much later a very bright light was seen, dawning from below.

"There's the moon, down there."

"The moon is down there?"

"That is my kingdom."

Tamàr was afraid. She did not want to descend, even though there were one hundred thousand little steps in the white rock.

"Come, come," said the beautiful young god.

Tamàr was crying. She did not want to leave the earth, her town where bells and birds chimed, her three sisters, her mother who prepared cooked fava beans to be eaten with vinegar and onions.

She was forced to go down there. It took a month and a day to reach the moon that was white marble in a black mantle.

"Ay, how fearful!" said Tamàr.

There was no one there. Above you could see our world which looked strangely green as it sailed through the sky.

The news got out and right away they told Taddeo Caldeo and his wife and daughters. The entire village ran to that deep ravine where in the very great distance the shining moon moved silently.

"O Tamàr, O Tamàr!" shouted her mother.

"O Tamàr, O Tamàr," called her father.

"O Tamàr, O Tamàr," said her sisters softly.

"O, our dear little Tamàr," cried the people.

The moon rocked like a cradle. It was the kingdom of the god of the moon, but it was a distant realm for the people up here, used to the hoe and the sod, the hen and the rabbit. That moon never returned, it sank under the earth. When a zephyr breeze rises up from below, you can hear the soft lament of that poor beautiful girl, lost in the sky. And you can hear: "Better up there, my dear mother, with black bread, than down here where the moon is an unsettling flame, without grain, without oregano, without fava beans." Amen. That's how the story ends.

The Boy with the Little Golden Horns

This Tamàr, daughter of a Judean farmer who every night in the deep darkness prayed to Adonài, managed to escape from the moon, where she had remained imprisoned with the King, going through dark dales and valleys. From there she gazed in silence at Mother Earth, who was shining, all in flower with climbing roses. She retraced her steps so far that she managed to find the long, long staircase carved into the lunar rocks that, with their stellar light, benumbed sight and sense. That's how it was.

She climbed back up, quite happy to find herself in her own land where, looking out from his castle, through his silver telescope, King Herod was watching the cobbler who was bending over his work, the blacksmith who was beating copper to make into swords, the potter who was quickly shaping clay into jars, the peasant who was harvesting olives on the holy mountain.

The King sees this girl who, because of the days and months spent traveling on the lunar mountain, had taken on a beautiful radiance. Even her little feet shone.

"Who is this?" he wonders.

And he takes a fancy to her, he who had at his beck and call all of the young ladies, adorned in pearls, of the Judaic realm. So... He had her summoned. She was afraid. She hides herself in a cave in the desert near the Dead Sea that in the night, with its shattered waves, sleeps.

He succeeded in having her captured by warriors in black mantles, with shields of sounding brass. And so the poor girl, who had left the unmeasured shining peace of the wandering underground moon, had two children by that King Herod, a boy with little golden horns on his head, and a girl with sapphires and precious gems in her hair.

Since she was a slave, she worked in the fields where thorn

bushes rise up next to fig trees and cinnamon trees. One day, her daughter, who was older now, said to her, "I have to do my business." "Go under an olive tree and do what you have to do."

A storm was brewing. It shook the vault of heaven with its thunder. The grasshoppers fled from the sheaves.

"Run," said Tamàr to her other little child, Ciro Giovanni, "and go call your sister. There are huge bolts of lightning in the sky."

The child Ciro Giovanni ran. He was seven years old. As he ran, his little golden horns, tinkling, struck his head. But the storm was fierce. The rain fell like terrible lances. It was a yellow rain, a dark rain. The two children lost their way. They hid themselves in a cave until they fell asleep. Day returned from the East, with a pitiless sun upon the earth.

"Oh, where are we?" asked the fearful boy.

"I don't know, my brother." They began walking again. They arrived at the Dead Sea that was sparkling in its solitude.

"Oh, what's this?" asked the boy. He had never seen sea or lake.

As swift as can be a shark appeared which leaped out of the water. The watery world shivered, as the shark carried the girl off into the waves. The boy cried loudly. The king's steward happened to pass by. He said to the child Ciro Giovanni: "Why are you crying?"

"I can't find my sister anymore, and I don't know where to go."

"Do you want to stay with me? You can watch the ducks, but you have to tend to them and make them eat, because they have to come back with full gizzards. Otherwise, you'll be in trouble."

"Alright," said the boy sorrowfully.

"What's your name?"

"Ciro Giovanni, but in my village they call me Perladoro."

The little golden horns on his beautiful forehead were shining with fright.

The boy went through those scorched lands with the ducks, but there was no grass, only stones and rocks with long blue veins.

"Now what will I do?" the boy said to himself. "There's no

grass to be found here. What can these ducks eat?" He began to cry. In a loud voice he called to his sister, lost in the Dead Sea. The little horns on his head were ringing.

"Dear little sister of mine, come, come, for they'll dig a grave for me if I don't make the ducks fill their gizzards. I can already hear them grinding the knives for the King's steward, who will cut my throat."

And from the depths of that Dead Sea his sister said to him, "Ask the shark, my dear little brother."

The boy begged the shark that was swimming in a sea cave. At a certain moment the shark felt compassion, and brought the sister up to the surface. When the two children saw each other, they embraced. Perladoro spoke: "I have become the duckherder and I have to make them eat if I don't want to be killed. But in these lands there are only rocks without grass."

The sister shook out her hair. Out fell many golden coins and the ducks filled their gizzards with them. The steward wondered why those ducks had full gizzards when all around in those woeful fields there grew no edible grass. He went to tell everything to the King, who was taking his pleasure seated under palm trees, where the sun was fading. It was a beautiful flickering sun.

"Can this be?" said the King. "Bring that boy here." The boy came in tears. He was afraid of the King, and he didn't know, poor Ciro Perladoro, that it was his father.

"Who are you?" asked King Herod.

"Perladoro."

He looked at the little horns shining on his head, and he thought: "They are signs of royalty."

"And your mother, who is she?"

"She is Tamàr."

The King understood and remained silent. An evil sorceress, watching the flight of crows toward the mountainous heights, had told him that a boy would usurp him, and that he, Herod, would lose all the riches of the kingdom. He said, "Go back to the sea and ask your sister what has to be done to release her."

Perladoro went back. The crickets were sleeping among the stones, and the crows were circling over those scorched lands.

"O darling sister, how can you be freed?"

A voice was heard rising from a whirlpool in the sea. It said, "O dear brother, it requires four of the strongest men with four steel hoes, for I am chained in the depths of the dark sea."

The King calls for help. He gives orders. The four strongest men arrive. They go to the sea, and break the chains with a great tremor.

Out steps the girl. Her hands were now blue, and even her hair had turned into beautiful shades of seaweed. The King was happy, for he had an idea.

"Call the steward."

He was a man with burning eyes and cruel nails. Even his heart was cruel.

"Your Majesty, at your command."

"Kill Perladoro and his sister."

First the boy died. His lost life struck the sea rocks like an arrow. The waves cried red tears. Then it was his sister's turn. With one blow, the sword cut off her head. Many golden pieces of coral scattered on the seashore.

They learned of it in the village. Everyone came running: the potter, the shoemaker, Uncle Michael Gabriel, the tailor with his waistcoat full of needles, Jaluna carrying an orange branch, Signora Arpina carrying a basket of grain, Farmer Giuseppe carrying olives in a bag. They brought Tamàr, the mother, who cried:

O my children, my lilies,
on the mountains of Galilee there is no peace.
The date tree is dying,
the fig tree is dying,
the camel is dying,
the world shrouds itself in black.

And the people replied in a chant:

Will the steppe flower again?
We have had our fill of absinthe.
Our life is bitterness,
We will have thorns, not beauty.
No more our couscous,
our red pepper, our bread.

The story ends here. They, with their arms and eyes and hearts of coral, are lost in the sea, and here we are alive in the shade.

The Twins as White as Lilies

Every morning the witch Zebaide rose up, darkening the sky and said, "Today I will destroy the earth. No trace of mankind will remain."

She scorned the green grass and the bread. She scorned the Holy Sabbaths of the poor villagers who, with scythes in their fists, worked all bent over blanching the earth with grain. The son of this witch, Giuseppe by name, looked down from his garden and saw a girl who was faithful, delicate, and wise, with hair like fine black thread. He fell in love with the dark skin of this beautiful girl, known as Proserpina. Learning of it, his mother said, "You're not going to marry her. She's not of your lineage."

This Giuseppe married her in secret at midnight, when day, because of the shadowy hour, lies still in the vault of heaven. Then Proserpina felt her eyes weaken, her hands as pliable as reeds, and she knew she was expecting a child. When the witch Zebaide learned of it, she felt an everlasting flame shoot throughout her entire person. The world darkened. Then she had a thought: she thought of having her daughter-in-law killed. She called to her, and said to her that she was to go to the center of the Island of Sicily, there where everything is rock, everything is black.

"Go to my sister to get some yeast for bread."

The girl went off, unsuspecting. Along the way she met a woman in tears, distressed and disheveled, who, kissing the ground, adored the dark stone fallen from the sky.

"Where are you going, beautiful dark-haired young woman?"

"I'm going to get some yeast."

"Be careful, be careful. Your mother-in-law wants to kill you. You will come across a dirty river, with putrid waters, and as soon as you see it, say: 'I'm very thirsty. What beautiful water there is here'. And drink a little. Then you will come across a dead wood with friendly dead birds, and further along, in terror you will see a famished wolf. Tell him: 'Take this bread. Eat'. Then you will find a donkey eating meat and a dog eating hay. Give the hay to the first one and the meat to the other."

The girl named Proserpina thanked her for so much kindness, and went away thinking of everything the Saracen woman had told her. She obeyed. She saw the river running in black arms of water, and she took some sips along the bank full of dead grass. In the woods, where the birds were singing, she met the wolf and gave him something to eat. To the dog she gave the meat and to the donkey who was pawing the ground she gave the hay. Her aunt the witch gave her the yeast. She was waiting for her at a window where basil and rue were growing.

On her return, as Proserpina was going along the marked path where the distant wind of the desert was speaking, she heard her mother-in-law say: "Dog, tear her to pieces!" But the dog replied, "No, she gave me some meat."

She arrives in the woods, where it was already evening. The trees – all asleep – were without eyes, and she heard: "Wolf, tear her to pieces!" But the wolf said, "No, she gave me something to eat."

She came again to the putrid river with its reddish-purple grass, where the sound of the water was a lament. The deceitful voice of the witch Zebaide said: "Drown her!" The river answered, "No, she drank from my sorrowing waters."

Let's leave the girl Proserpina and go to her mother-in-law who, from the tower, as dawn came proceeding in circles of quiet air, saw her daughter-in-law arriving along the road. Already at the sound of the morning bell, the peasant men and women were heading to work on their donkeys, or walking with their mattocks on their shoulders.

The witch was sunken in anger. She felt a hundred lions in her body.

So, the day arrived on which they were to deliver the girl of her baby. O beautiful river, o splendid flowering! The witch mother-in-law, as soon as she knew, leaned out of the window and brought her elbows down sharply on the window ledge, so that the girl suffered darting pains in her belly and was unable to give birth. The neighbor women realized what was going on. They were Saracen women, and they cried out: "Shame, O Zebaide! You don't want the girl to give birth!" In her anger Zebaide raised her elbows. Proserpina gave birth to two children, one male and one female.

The male child had a golden star on his forehead, the girl held a golden apple in her hand. They were signs of royalty that are passed on through the red rivers of the blood. Two really beautiful children, everyone gazed at them. Old Zebaide was dying of shrill jealousy.

Let's leave the mother and daughter-in-law to their destiny, the one frail from too much love, the other also frail, but from hatred. And let's go to the son who had gone off to the war that his enemies had declared. To his mother, before his departure, he had said, "Mother, I must go to war. I am entrusting Proserpina to you."

"Yes, my son, go. Let's hope that you win the war. As for Proserpina, I will take care of her."

Along with Prince Giuseppe had gone Orlando, Sansonetto, Oliver, and Rinaldo. They were all sparkling on account of their swords of silver, their breastplates of the finest diamonds. You could hear for a month and a day – further and further away – the pawing of their horses. Then nothing more was heard. The Prince learned that his wife had given birth to two children. It was said that to the boy she had given the name Salvatore and to the daughter, Anna. But the witch Queen Zebaide, in league with the midwife, placed two little lambs in the flowering cradle. On the forehead of one she branded a golden star, and she set a golden apple in the paw of the other. The witch had taken the two babies, Salvatore and Anna, twins by blood, and had entrusted them to the cook Giuda, whose eyelids were always wrinkled up because his very soul had doubts about his doings.

"Listen, my Giuda, take these babies, put them in a casket with a bottle of milk, and throw them into the sea."

"Into the sea, my Queen Zebaide? What a shame! They are so beautiful!"

But he obeyed. He went to the sea that was growing old with the boredom of knocking against a monotonous bank without trees.

Let's go back to Proserpina, who says: "Madam midwife, I want to see my children."

"Do you really want to see them?"

"And how could a person not want to see their own children?"

Zebaide came in a big red cloak and said: "You didn't have children."

"And what did I have?"

"Do you really want to see them? Here, you had two lambs. Good girl! What a fine one you turned out to be!"

The girl began to cry. Her thousand mother's hearts dried up within her. Zebaide said: "Now we'll write to my son. Let's see what he says and what he decides."

Her son the Prince, when he learned of the matter, felt himself grow faint. With a trembling hand, he wrote to his mother: "You were right. And now who am I? The father of two lambs? So, I'm a cuckold. You know what I say? Tie her to a stairway, and here is the order: 'Whoever comes by must spit in her face!' Give her a crust of bread and some water every day."

That poor Proserpina, out of a mother's love, had begun to nurse the two little lambs that, bleating, sucked at her crystal milk, but by order of the Queen she was bound to an olive tree that sprouted from the holy mountain called Carratabbìa. That horrible witch Zebaide gave the order that everyone in the kingdom had to spit in the face of Proserpina, mother of Salvatore and Anna. The people asked themselves: "Can it be that she has had two lambs? Let's go see." You could see them, like a line of ants, rising over the hill of Carratabbìa under the grey mantle of olive trees. Peasants came, barbers came, soldiers of other nations came. After a month and a day of that punishment, Queen Zebaide gave the order to shut her daughter-in-law up underground in a ditch, next to the Dead Sea which Proserpina, closed in down there, could hear turning in the night. Then the pomegranate flowered no more, the palm tree flowered no more. Even the fish in the sea were still.

Let's leave this poor buried girl, as a chill falls upon the earth, and let's go to the two children.

One day a miller, as he was brushing flour dust from his face, saw that far out, in the middle of the sea, a moving dot was shining. He ran to tell his wife.

"Marannedda, Marannedda, what's that in the sea near the shore?"

The woman looked. "What can it be, Pietro dear?"

"Bah. What shall I do?"

"Run. Go see."

He went out in a boat. He rowed to the middle of the throbbing waters. He reached that casket of death, and brought it to land.

"A dead man?" said his wife. "O God!"

They opened it.

"Let's see what there is."

They open a chest that we in Sicily call a *tabbutu* and inside they saw two children shining like the sun.

"Oh," said the miller's wife. "Oh, how beautiful they are!"

The woman was crying. "Innocent children. Is our world so evil?" She immediately sent her husband to our village. He came up by way of the rough path, in the piercing cold. He bought a she-goat. She gave milk to Salvatore and Anna. White liquid came out of the goat's udder. And so the children grew. Now they were six years old. One day, walking through the fields where the almond tree would not flower, and the blades of the prickly pear were dry, they began to dig into the earth with a small stick. As they were digging, they heard sighs. "What's underneath here?" said Anna.

"Ay, ay, ay."

Through the hole hollowed out between roots and dripping

black moisture they saw a woman.

"O Signora, Lady, what are you doing down there?"

"They have condemned me to stay here and I am dying of hunger. How very hungry I am! Would you give me some water?"

"Yes, we'll go get it."

The children ran, and got a pitcher. They filled it with the milk that gushed from the udder of the she-goat called Ciccina. The miller's wife asked, "Where are you going with that milk?"

"We're playing at making the grain grow. We're watering it with milk."

"Ha, ha," laughed the miller's wife. "Such innocence. Play, play."

They passed over frozen clumps of earth, over roots sticking out of the earth. They came to where their mother was interred. Down below she opened her mouth. The children poured the milk into the hole and so they fed their mother.

The next day, they asked the miller's wife: "Can you give us some bread? We're hungry."

"How can that be, when you've already had some milk?"

"O, give it to us, give it to us."

She gave them the bread fresh from the oven. It perfumed the very air like balsam. The children ran out through a little path full of rocks. In the distance the sea was sparkling, enclosed by the banks. They found the loosened earth, the hole, and the woman below opened her mouth, like a bird. They gave the bread to the interred woman. They fed her piece by piece.

"A little water," she cried.

And they gave it to her. As you see, they fed their mother every day, either with bread or milk or fish caught along the sea of Sicily.

Once the miller's wife asked herself: "And just where are these children going? Where? It's not right that they're always taking off."

She followed them, along with her husband, who went ahead. The pitcher of milk carried by the two children named Salvatore and Anna made a tinkling sound. The miller's step was light, even at the crossroads full of black stones. When they arrived, they saw the two little children, digging in the earth, which issued a lament.

"What is it?" they asked.

The two, brother and sister, cried and said, "Don't you see? There is a beautiful woman who is buried underneath here. Every day we feed her."

"O poor woman," said the miller's wife, looking through the hole where daylight penetrated in threads of flame. "Who are you?"

"I have become Queen of the earth, I, who earlier walked through meadows, over banks, in search of air. I have been condemned to lie here amidst roots and lumps of earth."

The miller's wife had a thought. She went with her husband to the Royal Palace which in our country is a castle set on a height where the dawn breaks in splendor. They made their request to a lady-in-waiting, "We wish to speak to the king."

"To the king?"

"Yes."

"He's off at war with all of his knights."

So. Three days went by. The sun rose and died. A sound was heard, like the tremendous blast of a horn. The victorious king arrived with 100,000 horses and knights. The miller and his wife returned with their request, "We want to speak to the King."

"You here again?" said the lady-in-waiting.

"We are asking you out of the divine love of our Triune God."

She goes and asks the King, "There are two ragamuffins who wish to speak with your Excellency."

"With me?"

"Yes."

"Show them in. Oh how tired I am of war."

"Lord, Lord and Prince, there's a lady buried in the earth."

"It was by command of my mother. And that's how it must be."

The cooks and the ladies prepared a huge feast, with couscous, sweets made of honey, figs, white, red, and blue prickly pears, and bread in round loaves – everything.

"I invite you all to dine," said the Prince. "Even those two children."

They went up to the castle with pictures on the walls, swords everywhere. Orlando removed his armor, dusty and bloodied. The two children had with them a warbler, one of those tiny ones you can hold in your fist. The King said, "Let's eat."

"We don't want to eat," said the two children. The star on the forehead of the boy was made golden by the midday shining on the roofs. The golden apple was a lamp in the hand of the girl.

"And why don't you want to eat? Don't you see all the dishes?"

"Before we eat we want our bird to give the order."

"What bird?"

They opened one hand, the left one that is bound to the heart with a thread of blood. You could see that tiny warbler.

"Ha, ha," laughed the King. "Birds talk? Since when?"

The little warbler, tiny as a mustard seed, said, "Don't eat unless you first free the woman who is under the earth. She is your mother."

The King gave a start. He looked at the two children and recognized the signs of royalty.

He rises up and shouts, "Treason! Treason!" Even Orlando, who was delighting in eating prickly pears sprinkled with cinnamon, leaped up.

The King: "Seize my mother Zebaide, traitorous witch. My wife did not have two lambs. I'm not a cuckold, but the father of these two children."

The cooks came, the attendants, and singers with guitars. The executioner came. Queen Mother Zebaide the witch was frightened. Her black heart fell. She said: "Have pity, son of a mother who did this for your own good. Pardon me."

"No, there's no pardon. Get a cauldron. Boil some oil and throw my mother in it."

It was the order of the King. Meanwhile, Orlando, Sansonetto, Rinaldo, and Malagigi went with the King. You could see caravans faraway in the desert. They freed Proserpina, who by this time had, you might say, feet made of roots. Even her poor hands were intertwined with green leaves. At the very same moment that they threw in the mother Zebaide, screaming, the earth was boiling. She is screaming even now, and at night that scream is tremendous. It reaches out as far as the dead waters.

A magnificent feast was held, with guitars, tambourines, and mandolins. The earth brought forth buds. The olive trees blossomed, the almond trees flowered, and along the banks of the sea wonderful campanula rose up.

The human race was happy, and here we are barefoot and without a thing.

The Lover Made of Honey

A cobbler lived alone with his daughter, for he did not wish to remarry after the death of his wife, who was lowered in a casket into a rock, also in tears, under the dying sun. But enough of this. Let's leave the poor dead woman who walks from path to path in the midst of the dark air, and go to the daughter named Granata who remained very unhappy as a result. She was seventeen. Her father said:

"O my daughter, listen to your father. Why are you sad? You receive so many proposals, and you don't want to marry. Say something."

"I want a favor from you."

"Yes, what do you want?"

"I want a room all to myself, and there inside, when at night the vault of heaven turns, you are to bring me a hundredweight of sugar, a hundredweight of honey, and a hundredweight of flour. Then I will stay closed in there for a year, a month, a day ..."

Her father asked, "What do you have to do, my daughter?"

"I'll tell you, and only you because you are my father. I want to make a husband for myself with my own hands, fashioning him according to my own ideas."

"So be it, daughter, do as you wish."

The father, by the name of Jacob, with the help of the donkey Rondello, brought sugar extracted from cane that grows near the desert, flour made of barley and wheat matured in tenderness on the heights, and honey made by bees sipping cinnamon, mallow, and catnip flowers.

Sparrows were singing on all the roofs of the village. Granata closed herself up in there, in the room. She fashioned a first young man, but she wasn't pleased. She fashioned a second, but she wasn't pleased. She fashioned a third. She wasn't pleased either with an eye, or the hands, or the heart that wasn't in place. And so on. Amen. The gracious girl was searching for her very own ideas.

The stated time passed, and only then was he ready, the silent youth made according to Granata's idea. She set the youth, made of sugar, honey, and flour, out in the sun to dry. The sparrows sang again. All the village was full of their song.

The girl breathed a clear breath into the mouth of that lover. He, no longer a puppet, became a splendid young prince. Her father, the cobbler Jacob, was happy.

Meanwhile a caravan was passing along the road. Going by on a camel was a gypsy woman, who dismounted in order to buy some bread. She saw that young man so splendidly alive. She looked up. The road was wet, and she fell and broke an arm.

"Evil fortune to you!" she said to Granata. "In order to find your husband, you will need seven pairs of iron shoes. You will have to walk seven years, and before you can find him, the fog, wind, and sun must enter your house together."

The girl laughed. She didn't believe it. She shut the window of the balcony where the day was sparkling. When she goes to open it, the noonday bells chimed, but she could no longer find the young man, whom she had named Sion. She took fright. She drew back. She said not a word. Her father asked her, "What's the matter, my Granata?"

She answered, "You know, father, a gypsy woman has put a curse on me." And she told him the whole story. She cried bitter tears.

"Remember, father, how handsome, sturdy and well formed my fiancé was?"

"Yes, my girl."

"Now, father, in order to find him again, I need seven pairs of iron shoes, and I must go wandering throughout the earth. Oh, my dear father!"

"Don't be frightened."

Her father, Jacob the cobbler, got hold of stones black with iron. He broke them up, and one by one he made seven pairs of shoes. His daughter went off. Her father cried. There were no sparrows on the roofs in our village.

This Granata went through lands where it was hot, so hot that the stones boil. In the distance one could see Mt. Calvary with its crown of olive trees. On the other side of the Dead Sea, she met three monks.

"Daughter, where are you going?" they asked.

"In search of my ill-fortune." They felt sad. They knew that the body is mortal and that after our death a hundred spirits rise up. One said, "Daughter, I give you this hazel nut." The other, with a reddish beard, "I give you this almond." The last, with one lame foot, said, "I give you this walnut."

Granata resumed her journey. She came to a large town. She climbed to the top of the mountain. Out of hunger she wanted to open the walnut, and – oh, what a wonder – inside she found a tiny gold loom.

She began to say, almost singing, "Who would like a loom of gold? Who would like it?" The old women, roosters at their feet, looked at her. There was a loud burst of wind. The ladies-in-waiting heard that loud cry, and they told the Queen.

"Queen, good Queen, there's a girl who is selling a gold loom."

"Call her to me, call her."

Granata came, but she was pale as mist because she had learned that the Queen had bought and adopted as her son none other than her own Sion, made of sugar and honey. The King had fathered a thousand sons by many women, including Mary of Nazareth, but he had ordered them slaughtered because he was afraid of being usurped.

The ladies asked, "How much money do you want?"

"I don't want money."

"So what do you want?"

"A favor."

"What?"

"I would like to sleep tonight with the son of the Queen, young Sion."

They ran off.

"Queen, Queen, she wants to sleep with your son Sion in exchange."

The Queen looks at the loom. It was so small you could scarcely see it in the well of one hand. The sun shimmered above. The Queen fell in love with that loom. She had never seen anything like it, not even remotely similar.

"So be it, so be it."

But she thought of a trick. She calls Mafalda, lady-in-waiting, and says to her, orders her, to give young Sion a drink of opium.

"Drink it, drink it, Prince," went Mafalda.

The young man drank. His soul sank into sleep. Little by little he ended up in a sea of dreams. At night, as agreed, the young Granata went to bed with the man she had created according to her own ideas. She took him in her arms. She called to him in fleeting words, honeyed words. "Sion, son of the King, I made you with my own hands. I fashioned your eyes, your forehead. I sweetened your heart without being able to get any pleasure from it."

The young man was asleep. He was sailing on the waves of sleep, and didn't hear.

Day came. The cock crowed. The lady-in-waiting came: "Now you may go." Granata went away, saddened, through streets full of sunshine.

She cracked open the almond, and found there a spindle of gold. She called out again in the streets, "Women, who would like a spindle of gold?"

The Queen heard her as she was gathering drops of incense from the trees in her garden that put forth leaves on the ancient oaks.

"Call her to me, call her."

"Here she is, Queen."

The gold spindle was as small as coral. The early morning faded before its glimmer.

"I don't want money, Queen, but I want to sleep tonight with your son Sion."

She agreed. Evening came. The bat appeared. The Hebraic people, seeing the sun no longer, became melancholy. The girl took in her arms again the young man made of honey. She sang lullabies to him, saying: "The one who made you with her own hands / Loves you with true love and does not deceive you."

He was drugged, so he didn't hear her. He sighed the moist sigh of sleep.

Day came. It dawned with the beautiful shining star. She was sent away.

Let's leave Granata and go to the Queen's neighbor, who was named Jaluna. Every night she heard the pain of the girl who, with a very clear voice, sang to young Sion. She called to the Prince from her low balcony – she was a poor woman, Jaluna – and she said, "Your Majesty, for two nights I've been hearing a girl singing and crying."

"And what does she say?"

"She says: 'Sion, I made you with sugar and honey in accordance with my own ideas'."

"Ah," Sion said to himself, "this evening I'll take care of things."

And so, he did not drink the opium. He did not touch the graceful beaker with the Cedars of Lebanon stamped in finest silver. Granata had cracked the hazelnut, finding there a shuttle of gold that gleamed so intensely it was reflected in a thousand streams.

"What is this light?" asked the Queen. And meanwhile, Granata sang, "Who would like this shuttle of gold? Who would like it?"

The Queen bought it. When Granata took the young man in her arms, he asked her, "Who are you?"

"My name is Granata. I fashioned you with my own hands, according to my own ideas."

Sion became frightened, he looked at her in complete wonderment; then he embraced her.

Day came again, white and red, turning the vault of heaven. The lady Mafalda returned and said: "Beautiful young woman, you may go." The young man replied: "No, lady-in-waiting, *you* may go. This is my wife. She herself fashioned me of sugar and honey."

He took the steed that whinnied. He left for the temple, to adore their God, who was a great black calf.

The Queen was frightened. Learning everything, she felt weak, as though she had no heart left. She sent the message through the town crier, who sounded his horn through the streets:

"Come back, come back, Sion. Come back, come back, Granata. The Queen pardons you and makes you sovereigns of the Hebraic land."

To the joy of everyone, a great feast was held. Even the Dead Sea, that stretched out desolate over the desert, roared. The lame came and ate honey. The woman without breasts came and ate citron. The old man without his right leg came and drank new wine with Armenian bread. The black child came and cried at seeing figs, prickly pears, and red pepper on focaccia bread.

Jacob the cobbler of our village, Minèo, went to that land where the storks fly. He was made prince, but he only knows how to use twine and an awl, and goes on making shoes for poor old people.

There they are, married and happy, and here we are, so far away.

Palmuzza and the Bogeyman

A poor stone-breaker went from quarry to quarry, through valleys and mountains, to uproot rocks from their roots. About midday he would rest among the solitary shadows. He would return only once a week to the village to celebrate the Sabbath, with unleavened bread, prayer, and deep sleep. He had three daughters who would bid him farewell whenever he headed off again for the cliffs, paths, and dried rivers. One day, seeing that her two sisters were watching from the attic as their father got smaller and smaller, as though sucked up by the light, the oldest said, "What are we waiting for? Let's get to work."

"Yes," answered the other two.

Elena, the oldest, said, "I will spin with the distaff and spindle." The second one, Giacobbina, said, "I will embroider a carpet of agave fiber." The youngest said, "I will read the story of King Pennanculo."

The oldest spun, the second embroidered, the youngest read the story of the King. The day flashed full on the roofs. The oldest said, "If I were to marry the King's cook, with just one match I would prepare a huge meal." The second, who was making her way through a wood embroidered in gold threads, said, "If I were to marry the coachman of King Pennanculo, with just one skein of silk I would make him a suit of clothes."

The youngest one, as she was traveling along dewy paths and fresh hoarfrost in her book, said: "If I were to marry the son of King Pennanculo, I would give him twins, one male, with the sun on his forehead, and one female, with the moon in her hand."

"Ha, ha," laughed the sisters. But they were jealous. They felt what seemed like a biting that gnaws at the flesh. They said, "This thread to be woven is too long. We'll have to dig a hole for it to go through."

Meanwhile, through the narrow street of black chimneys, came King Pennanculo. With him came his dignitaries, one with a white mare, one with an elephant, one on a camel. The King, hearing the girls laugh, gave the order to stop. He listened. He heard those girls laugh like birds among green flowers. He laughed and said, "They're something, the daughters of Peppi the stone-breaker. They want to marry my cook, my coachman, and my son, Crown Prince Saul."

Let's leave the King on his black horse with his thoughts (he can wait), and go back to the two sisters who are digging a hole in the floor. The oldest resumes spinning, and the thread fell into that hole.

"And who's going to go down there?" she said.

"I'll go down," said Palmuzza, with a light spirit. While she was descending into the black hole, the older sister said to Giacobbina, "Cut the thread." The thread was cut, and it snapped back as though whipped. The young girl fell into the ditch.

"Run, run," the two sisters said faintly, but no one could hear that tiny little voice.

The sister, fallen into the ditch, grew frightened. She shouted, looking up, and wells of tears sprang up in her eyes. But seeing that down below everything was dark, she started to walk until she came to a garden adorned with walnut, hazelnut, and black pepper trees.

"Oh what a beautiful garden," she said.

There was a palace. Trees and prickly pears blossomed around it. Palmuzza enters. She sees a chair in a room, but she heard a loud noise like thunder that explodes in the sky. She hides herself under the chair.

With furrowed eyebrows and the smell of seawater, in came the bogeyman, who sat down on the chair and let out a fart that roared through the arches. The girl screamed in fright. The bogeyman bends down. He sees her, and says, "Aha! With one fart I've brought forth a daughter. With one fart I've brought forth a daughter." Then he asked, "What's your name?"

"Palmuzza."

"Palmuzza, my daughter. You should know one thing. There are many beautiful things inside here – sapphires, sea stones, and lunar rocks. Everything is yours, but don't open the door to that room."

"Why, my dear father?"

"I can't tell you."

Palmuzza couldn't be persuaded that she was not to open that door, which was made of iron metal and which rang if you struck your little finger against it.

She talked herself into opening it. It wasn't easy with all its locks in different shapes – some triangular, some square, some rectangular. What did she find? It was an empty room. Melancholy echoed from wall to wall. Since there was a chair in dark gold, almost as dark as black pitch, Palmuzza understood that the bogeyman closed himself up in that room whenever he was tired of the world, of the noise of the rumbling wind, of the knights who went out in search of fortune. But enough. Now in one corner, what does she find? Three skeins of thread, like little hazelnuts: one was red, one blue, and one white as the wings of a dove. She re-set the thirty-three locks; it wasn't easy.

Her father the bogeyman came home, and called to her:

"Palmuzza, Palmettina, will you let down your hair? / Your father is coming. / Palmuzza Caterinella, will you let down your hair? / Your father is coming."

It was in his nature to amuse himself by changing her name. He sat down very wearily, and said, "Oh, what a scent of human flesh."

Palmuzza: "O father, do you come from the coasts with your nostrils full? / Or do you come from the mountains with your nostrils like baskets?"

"No, I smell the scent of human flesh."

"Or maybe you smell my flesh?"

"Oh how thoughtless, it's true! But I have such a longing to eat human flesh."

And he looked at her with wistful eyes. Just as well Palmuzza played the strings of a harp and put him to sleep.

Naturally the girl was afraid. One day or another he might forget that she was his Palmuzza and eat her up.

Once he was sad. His reddish gaze turned very pale. He had no desire to see the parrot jump on the branches, nor to see the sun bow down in the evening. He said, "Palmuzza, my daughter, I want to leave you well off."

"What are you saying? I don't understand you."

"You must now do what I tell you: you must kill me."

"Kill, my father?"

"Yes, because if I want to, I can be a dog, I can be a king, I can be a divine leopard."

"Oh father, what kind of ideas are you making up?"

"I'm not making trouble, nor making it up. You know that if any living being dries up, it gets sick. If you destroy the umbilical cord, our every desire ceases."

Palmuzza didn't understand.

"Kill me and you'll be rich, but you have to always live with the memory of me. If you turn traitor, I can be born again. Worse for you!" Palmuzza was crying. She said: "I will do as you wish."

She cut off his head, which fell to the floor in a red burst, its eyes still shaking in fear. She sawed off his legs, which painted the palace with blood. She cut open his belly to draw out the intestines that rumbled like a war horn. She did as her father the bogeyman had told her. She wound one intestine around her neck. With the blood she painted the walls, and with the arms and feet she made supports for the tables.

When Palmuzza had done all these things, she became more beautiful, with her hands like fronds and her face like roses of the field. The intestine wound around her neck became a necklace of brilliant diamonds. Even the sun, coming in through the pale shade of a wood, grew frightened. The tables were of gold, the house shone like a bright shield.

"Oh what riches!" said Palmuzza. "If only my sisters knew."

But she could not leave that house, which reached up from underground as far as the surface of the earth, like a castle with towers,

She cried: "What shall I do? Am I always to stay shut up in here?"

The peacock passed by and said: "O, poor Palmuzza, you are rich, but your destiny is like that of the eel, who must remain in the water." The falcon went by, flying high over the cliffs, and said, "O Palmuzza, you shine like a star, but your lips are not singing."

One time she heard the trotting of horses. Stones rolled down from the high mountain onto that castle buried in the depths.

"Help! Help!" shouted Palmuzza.

Prince Saul was passing by. Behind him rode seven knights and the apostles Peter, Paul, and John. They were singing a gloomy litany that rang out in the still air. Palmuzza listened:

> Steep, rugged peaks, don't you know that
> Our God, Horse, Bull, Lamb,
> Is wondrously made of stones?
> Praise to him: he flashes, he walks.
> His are the thunderbolts of the world.

Palmuzza leaned out from the balcony that was under the earth. From a ditch King Saul saw her.

"And who are you, you down there?"

"O good man, save me. I am Palmuzza. My father is no longer the bogeyman, but Peppi the stone-breaker."

"Peppi the stone-breaker?"

The Prince gave the order to stop. The holy apostles said:

"Down below in the earth are evil spirits. Our God is a horse-light, a lamb-light."

"Quiet, all of you! Here I give the commands."

Slowly, slowly the young King descended into the solitary valley. A torrent flowing from the rocks assaulted him. A serpent attacked his ankle. He saw that girl, how beautiful she was! He burned with love.

"I wish to marry you."

"You wish to marry me?"

She told him about the three skeins.

"Get them. Let's escape. Who do you think is going to come to this dead valley?"

She took the three skeins. They escaped.

But in doing this Palmuzza had turned traitor to the bogeyman, and out of the valley came a flash, and the bogeyman began to be reborn. The tables shrank back, and he had his legs. The house became pale, and he had his blood. The necklace of shining stones fell from Palmuzza, and he had a long, long intestine.

"O Palmuzza, O Palmuzza," he shouted, "traitorous daughter, where are you going? Where are you?"

The girl, in order to climb back into the valley, had gone up a stairway of silk that the seven knights had thrown down to her. King Saul followed her up the stairway. The holy apostles said: "The underground is a burning forge, and it is full of devils and serpents. Kill Palmuzza, kill her."

King Saul gets on his horse, behind Palmuzza.

"Let's hurry. Come on!"

Palmuzza turned, she said: "Oh, my father the bogeyman is overtaking us. What shall we do?"

"Throw down the white skein."

She threw it down. By threads and strands, in streams and brooks, it formed the very wide arm of a very blue lake. The sorcerer got off the horse on which he had passed through those sad fields. He began to swim. He saved himself.

"Stop, Palmuzza-Caterinella, stop, traitorous daughter!"

They galloped through the air that resounded with reins and hooves.

"He is overtaking us," said Saul.

The girl throws down another skein. Immediately it created a foam that covered the hill. It swelled up around the oak trees, and burst into bubbles from the heat.

The bogeyman could not swim, for he would slip, so he began clambering up protruding branches, rocks, and around ravens that wished to help him. And so... He got through.

"Oh, oh," said Palmuzza. "He's at our heels."

The seven knights protected Saul and the girl with their unsheathed swords. She hurls down the red skein; it caught fire and burst into flames. From a small ball it became a huge ball of fire. A thousand sparks shot straight up to the shining sun. The wizard could not manage to get through it. Dying, in flames, he said: "I am the light of the world. I will always shine. You, traitorous daughter, once your youth passes, will be the ashes that I leave behind."

Let's go back to the knight-King who began walking. He didn't give the slightest thought to the holy apostles who had also died in the fire.

"Where do you live?"

"There," replied Palmuzza.

So they went there. They found the poor tearful woodcutter. He had been crying for seven years. Her sisters had become more beautiful. They felt more free from the time Palmuzza was no longer there.

"Knock, knock."

"Who is it?"

"It's Palmuzza."

"Palmuzza, my daughter?"

"Yes, father."

Her father ran to her and embraced her. And: "Who is this knight?"

"Prince Saul."

"Oh, and what does he want with us?"

"Do not be afraid. I, Prince Saul, wish to marry your daughter."

"My daughter? But I am a poor woodcutter."

But afterwards, King Pennanculo, happy to see his son again, said to him: "I give you Palmuzza as your wife, but she has to keep her promise."

"Yes, Majesty, I will give Your Majesty twins."

"And your sisters?"

"They will do what they promised."

First it was Elena's turn who, in the kitchen, among the pots, spits, and burning fires, with only one match prepared a dinner of couscous, pepper, honey, and cinnamon sweets.

"Brava, brava!" said the dignitaries.

The second girl, Giacobbina, with one length of silk made a jacket, pants, and cloak. The first one married the cook, the second the coachman.

Then it was Palmuzza's turn. She became pregnant. Afraid of not keeping her promise, she prayed to the Sun, she prayed to the Moon when it shone at night, to grant her the favor. Otherwise, oh, shame, oh, sorrow!

At the moment of birth, King Pennanculo became worried and called the midwife who, riding a donkey, came with her instruments.

"Oh, come, come, for the sake of the bountiful Son!" they had said to her.

Palmuzza had twins. On the forehead of the boy was the sun that spread out along his temples in waves of light. The girl was born with the moon in her hands, that shone in threads and specks on the bone combs of the ladies-in-waiting.

"What sparkling things there are in the world!" they all sighed.

King Pennanculo was happy. His son very happy. The woodcutter cried in remembrance of his wife buried in the shadowy world. The knights held war games. The trumpets of the entire kingdom blared.

And here we are, waiting for the earth to give us grain and fava beans for our happiness.

The Girl in the Tree

This Palmuzza – said the old Centamore woman who told me these stories – made love to Crown Prince Saul only when the nights were blue, with the trill of the nightingale in the woods, and so she had only male children. The first was Pennanculo, named after his paternal grandfather, the second Peppi, after his maternal grandfather. The third would become St. Nicola. The fourth was Simone, the fifth Eliodoro, the sixth Settimo. One day these young boys said to their mother: "We want a sister." Unhappy, she replied, "Can't you see that God doesn't send me one?"

Palmuzza became pregnant again. She went walking in the garden, among palm trees and eucalyptus trees, with her ladies, who fluttered fans edged in silver. The kingdom awaited the birth with great expectation. But another male child was born, hale and hearty. He was named David, and would become St. David. The brothers grew sad, and they decided to go away. As the seven brothers were walking, they came across an old hermit who was walking through the dry leaves of the fields. Seeing them, he made a sign, and they turned into birds.

Let's leave these boys to their fate as birds flying over endless yellow paths, and go to their mother, Palmuzza, who had said to her sons, "If I have a daughter, I will order all the trumpets of the kingdom to sound out the news."

After giving birth to seven male children, another four years went by before she became pregnant again. This time she had a female child, white as the moon, with the breath of roses in her mouth.

Her mother Palmuzza was so very happy. In her thoughts she said, "Now my seven sons, pillars of the kingdom, will return."

The trumpets were sounded, as the sad story goes, but the bird-sons, floating in the air, heard nothing. The years went by, and time, you know, is made of three things: the essence of the soul, invisible particles born all around, bitter gall and dying matter.

A woman had warned the King, "Majesty, your daughter will meet with a terrible fate at the age of eighteen." He took fright. He never let his daughter, Mariella-Selisia-Ectàbana, go out. He made her grow up in the garden, which was a large stretch of red land. Fig trees grew there, and pumpkins with very beautiful low-growing flowers. There were palm trees. Agave plants rose up, the long flowers of the scilla, the mandrake. As for animals, there were the whitest of white hares, peacocks, roosters, blue serpents, martens, pheasants, everything you could imagine. At a certain place below the earth ran a stream that was sweet to hear. There was a huge walnut tree with branches and leaves that tinkled like silver.

And so the girl grew up. She was eighteen and a beauty, but no one except the ladies of the court had ever seen her. One day she said to her mother, "Dear mother, I am going to take a walk in the garden."

"Go on, my daughter."

She went off. Seeing her, the trees laughed and made merry. She sees the walnut tree and climbs up it. Sitting down, she began to embroider a royal cloak in gold.

Oh, how alone she was, poor girl!

As she was making gold with her eyes, along came the maidservant Daria to fetch some water. In the stream she saw a truly beautiful image, and she thought it was she herself.

"Oh what a beauty I am!" she said to herself. "As beautiful as this and I'm fetching water?"

She snatched the pitcher and smashed it.

"And why have you come back without water?" said the Queen.

"Why, I am beautiful. Too beautiful just to go fetch water."

"You, beautiful?" the ladies in attendance laughed. "You're ugly. You've got a pox-ridden face, twisted legs, and no tits."

She takes up another pitcher and goes again to the water. In the river that ran in quiet waves, she again saw the image.

"Oh how truly beautiful I am."

And she smashed the pitcher.

The Queen: "But how many pitchers are you going to break in one day? Do you want to send the kingdom to ruins?"

Again she goes back, and her footprints sank deeper into the earth. Again she gazed into the river, she touched the waves with her hands, making one image into one thousand images, and sees herself flowing out into the entire garden. But then she heard laughter.

"Ha, ha, ha!"

She looked up and saw Mariella.

"Oh, is that you in the tree, little Queen?"

"I'm here embroidering in gold."

"Yikes, who knows how long you've been up there! Get down, get down, in a little bit the sun will die, it won't sparkle anymore."

"I've been here for three days."

"Get down, get down. At least let me brush your hair." The walnut tree was yellow. Leaves lay at the feet of the princess. The garden was turning yellow.

She got down. All around her was the scent of a strong fragrance.

So Daria brushed the girl's hair, and as she did so, the very strands of her hair began crying. With no one to see her, Daria stuck a big pin into Mariella's nape. She was so jealous of her beauty. The body of Mariella, all sugar and honey, lay resting on the ground. Her soul flew off like a nightingale.

The maidservant was happy. Then, seeing Mariella dead, her crystal beauty untouched, she fled. She jumped over the wall and lost herself in a crowd of people. Some were selling fried pastries in the streets, and others porridge with honey.

For seven days Palmuzza waited for her daughter. She knew that she was working on her embroidery. She went to look for her, but found no one. The grass had covered her. In the evening, the star Sirius was reflected in the little river. The Pleiades were there, crying in the waters. A proclamation was issued: "Whoever finds our daughter Mariella will receive 100,000 loaves of bread, and 100,000 leather bottles of wine."

No one knew what Mariella looked like, so no one could find her. Winter came to that distant foreign land. The snow fell, covering over her beautiful body. In the temples they prayed. In penance, the Sisters in their black vestments recited the "Salve Regina." Scenes of the Nativity were set up all over the country. The caves were filled with she-goats and little donkeys.

Palmuzza cried. She had no peace. The Wise Men came. There were seven of them, and each of them, traveling on their donkeys and suffering from the cold, carried a bird as a gift. The hooves of their donkeys resounded on the pavement.

"Behold our gift," they said to the Queen, now grown old from her heart's sufferings.

Their gifts were the fish-bird, the lamb-bird, the sparrow-bird, the kite-bird, the partridge-bird, the bird of Paradise, and the bird-without-a-name. The serving women offered the Wise Men blancmange and fried pastries with honey. The entire kingdom was in mourning. By order of King Saul they did not even celebrate the passion of Jesus, who went up to Calvary carrying the heavy cross.

"If my daughter is dead, Jesus is dead, too. There will be no more religion in my lands."

Meanwhile, the cook saw a nightingale arrive, trembling in the terrible cold. It perched on the window, and, to the wonder of the servant, it said:

> Cook, cook in the kitchen,
> What are the King and Queen doing?
> They in the chamber and in the kitchen,
> And I a poor miserable thing.

After saying this, it flew off. This happened every time the blessed sun was about to rise, leaving the wide valley where it sleeps with the chirping crickets. The dawn was white. The cook reported to the king: "Majesty, My King, every morning a nightingale comes, perches on the windowsill, cries out, and says: "Cook, cook in the kitchen, / What are the King and Queen doing? / They in the chamber and in the kitchen / And I a poor miserable thing."

"This doesn't seem right," said the King.

"What shall we do, Majesty?"

"Get some glue and spread it on the windowsill. We have to capture that nightingale. I want to put it in a cage."

The cook obeyed. The nightingale, no longer able to fly, was completely terrified. The King was happy. He said in a shrill tone to his wife, "We've caught the nightingale."

Then what happened? How did it please God who, from distant lands, infinite and serene, sits in contemplation of our earth as it turns and turns and turns? The seven birds of the Wise Men came, the kite first. With their claws they freed the nightingale.

"After them, run!" shouted King Saul.

The priest came. A fellow named Moses came. The soldiers came, with swords and resounding guns. They ran after that cloud of birds that flew in the shining rain, through the branches of the garden. All of the birds perched on the walnut tree without branches, in the snow that was melting in the rain. The birds sang, but it was a song of lament that even the Pleiades, rising in the stream, heard. The King stumbles and falls.

"Majesty, did you hurt yourself?" the soldiers asked. He was old, poor thing.

"I feel something below me. It is soft and warm."

They go to brush off the snow, and there they saw the beautiful immaculate body of his daughter.

"My daughter?" shouted the King. "Buried under a frozen mantle that she herself was sewing with golden threads?"

At the sight of her, the birds, who were the seven brothers, shed their feathers and claws, shed their birdsong in the soft falling of snowflakes and water. It happened in an instant. There was a sudden flash.

"Soldiers, are you firing without my orders?" cried the King.

But no, the seven brothers had turned into young men. One was Pennanculo, one was Peppi with the big hands, one turned into Nicola, the fourth Simone, the fifth Eliodoro, one was Settimo, the last was David. They lifted up the body of their sister. They offered it to the walnut tree that bent down its bare branches. The nightingale perched on top of the tree. Mariella-Selisia-Ectàbana was reborn.

The father and daughter embraced each other very tightly.

"How ever did this happen, daughter?"

"This pin, this pin."

A lamp was lit in every window of every house in that distant country. Trembling, afloat on the water of the stream, ran the star Sirius and the Pleiades.

The Bird with the Blue Feathers

Inasmuch as the vault of heaven is immortal, it should inspire purity, humility, and love. If it please our God Macone, I will tell you the story of Manfredo and Corradino, sons of King Frederick. One day, the king, who liked to go hunting, issued a proclamation. The town crier, going throughout the realm of our land Sicily, where summer was blazing, proclaimed: "Whoever finds the bird with the blue feathers will receive as a prize one-hundred times one-thousand *carloni, tarì,* and *papetti* of gold."

Even the rook in the woods repeated the proclamation. Hearing it, many young men set out. Corradino – who wasn't even fifteen years old – said to his mother: "Queen Mother, have you heard the proclamation?"

"And you, son, what does it have to do with you?"

"It has a lot to do with me. I am going."

The other brother, Manfredo – he wasn't even twenty – said: "Our blonde Empress, I am going too."

They were mad with desire to find the bird with the blue feathers. It was flying over the sea at the spot where whirlpools rise up. The waves there have no tenderness, but are immeasurably full.

In short, they set out, the older son on his wild red horse, the younger son on his white one. They passed through sad fields, bare trees, serpents, and rocks. And so at last they arrive. The two boys go into the waters, which in that arm of the sea were called the waters of the Seni. Far off they saw the bird in its blue beauty. The waves were full of shadows. They swam. The bird stayed low. The two brothers circled round it. They reached for it with their young arms. Corradino managed to grab it. He felt roses spring up in his eyes. Manfredo felt full of serpents and thorns.

"Ah," he said, "You've got it? Now you will have all that

money."

Now Manfred was a heartless brother, son of a different mother, so when Corradino gets out of the waters of the Seni, he kills him, and buries him at a place in the woods where bramble bushes and hawthorn hid him.

That poor child never again returned home. And the mother asked her stepson, "And your brother, where is he?"

"He hasn't returned?"

"No. He must be among the forests and the stone piles."

"I don't know. Here's the blue bird."

The King was amazed and frightened. He said, "All the money is yours."

They waited for Corradino, but he did not return. The order was given to search for him. The knights set out, the soldiers set out, even the Marshall set out. No one could find him.

"Queen, he is nowhere to be found."

"O my poor son."

She became as sad as a flower closed up in a forest. Some time passed, three years. Once a shepherd boy with eleven she-goats and a dog was passing near the sea. The dog smelled a stench. He dug in the earth. Out came some bones in the fuming ancient air.

"Oh, it is some bones," said the shepherd boy. He didn't know that they were human bones, sad and dead. He made himself a whistle out of one of the bones. He put it in his mouth, and that whistle sang in a lament:

> O shepherd boy who holds me in his arms,
> I was killed in the waters of the Seni
> for capturing the blue bird.
> And it was my older brother.

That shepherd boy, poor wretch, became confused. He went up to his village and told his father.

"You're making it all up. Let me hear it."

The bone whistle sang its sorrowful song.

O shepherd who holds me in his arms,
I was killed in the waters of the Seni
for capturing the blue bird.
And it was my older brother.

The shepherd was upset. He ran to the Marshall and said: "Sir Marshall, this whistle speaks."

"Ha, ha, ha! Let me hear it."

And the whistle began to play.

He heard the same voice:

O Marshall who holds me in his arms,
I was killed in the waters of the Seni
for capturing the blue bird.
And it was my older brother.

The Marshall galloped on his horse to the palace of King Frederick.

"Our Empress Queen, news, grave news."

"What is it, Marshall?"

The Queen put the bone whistle in her mouth. She heard a wail that tore through her beautiful golden hair.

O dear mother who holds me in her arms,
I was killed in the waters of the Seni
for capturing the blue bird.
And it was my older brother.

Everyone was frightened, even the King. He said:

"It is not right, this mournful song."

They set out for the waters of the Seni. They rode for a day, a night, and a day. They dug in the exact spot indicated by the trembling hand of the shepherd boy. They found a young white skeleton that looked silver, without its vital heart.

"High treason!" said King Frederick. "High treason!"

He gave the order to take Manfredo, to bring him with his feet bound. But he was faraway, fighting the Saracens, who were falling back to the borders battered by the sea that pounded against the white sand. The Queen did nothing but cry, her pain was so great. She fell sick and died. The autumnal shadows spread out over the land. Manfredo's war horn knew no peace. It is said that this young man was killed in a fierce battle. An arrow passed through his heart. At night, mercenaries walking with torches carried his body, their brave heads lowered as a sign of perpetual mourning. King Frederick, by the will of God, remained alone, old and tired. And when the sun set in the depths of the sea, to dispel his melancholy he played the bone whistle that kept repeating, as if time were immovably still, without ever having changed course:

> *O dear father who holds me in his arms,*
> *I was killed in the waters of the Seni*
> *For capturing the blue bird.*
> *And it was my older brother.*

The story is told, the story is written. The King is all alone in his great castle, and here we are in our poor house.

Pelosetta

Once upon a time in Sicily there lived King Carlo, a fierce warrior who, in his journeying over the lands, was followed by the dark sign of the Scorpion that shines black in a thousand images.

This King had a son, Ruggero by name, who was warlike and daring in battle. But he had become used to pleasures, to balls, to playing at dice, to long rides under the moon, whether bright or dark. His mother was a lady of high lineage and intelligence who lived in a most genteel fashion, honored by her French subjects. She had for her servant a Saracen girl who lived in the stall with the donkey Rondello, along with the hens and the rooster Cuccuvì. Every morning, after the ladies had set his silver sword at his side, Ruggero called to the servant girl:

"Pelosetta, Pelosetta, bring Your Master his eggs."

"Yes, Master."

They were yellow eggs, sometimes with tiny little diamond-shaped yolks. For they were from royal hens.

One day Pelosetta replied: "No, Master, Prince Ruggero, I can't come up. I have to go for water."

She went to the emerald fountain amidst the red rays of the sun. On her return, Ruggero, in his helmet adorned with a white eagle, said to her: "You know, Pelosetta, tomorrow I am going to a ball."

"Can I come too?"

"Ha, ha, blackened with ashes as you are? Never, never."

The girl didn't reply. She felt her heart dry up. She went again to the water with her pitchers set inside the chests on the back of the donkey Rondello. Crying along the sun-filled road, she was filling the two pitchers with tears when suddenly she felt the sweet breath of a voice: "Pelosetta!" She saw no one. The turtledove in the tree went "glug, glug."

"Who is calling me?"

Suddenly there appeared, in a perfumed breath of air, a very beautiful woman.

"O Madonna!" said the Saracen servant girl, crying.

"Don't cry, I will help you. I will give you a gown all covered in braid, gold braid, and a pair of shining emerald earrings. When your master Ruggero of the shining white eagle says to you: 'I am going to a party, Pelosetta', you must make believe it's nothing to you, and then dress yourself in these veils and skirts of mine."

After eight days, Ruggero, his eyes like the light of day, again said: "You know, Pelosetta, I am going to a party tonight."

"I hope Your Majesty enjoys himself. I'm staying here with the rooster, the hens, and the donkey Rondello."

Off he goes. His horse is heard trotting over the scorched lands. Pelosetta immediately dresses herself in the gown all covered with gold braid. She looked like the Madonna and a dazzling star.

"What do I do now?" she asked herself. The rooster crowed, the hen replied. The fairy came.

"Here is a flying horse, Pelosetta, and a coachman."

The horse, with a mane white as snow, had a bit that shined and hooves that were quick. He flew over roofs, courtyards, over the peasants asleep on the threshing-floor, guarding the grain already winnowed by the sleepy turning of the donkeys. She arrives at the party in a palace – let's say it's in Palagonia, which is a village near ours, with gardens of orange and almond trees. Everyone gazed at her. An old man said: "Oh, what divine beauty! It gladdens one's eyes; it cures one's ills."

When Ruggero saw her, he set down his helmet. He felt like he was going mad.

"Dance with me, my lady."

They danced the polka and the mazurka. Faraway the herds of oxen crossed the plain. The trembling oranges ripened. While they were dancing, she steals a watch, set with rubies and topaz, from Prince Ruggero. Making up an excuse, she leaves. She runs off.

She flies away on the horse, over softly sleeping plants, over the torrent, waterless and in pain. Ruggero notices that his watch is missing.

"That woman stole it from me! How could I be so stupid?"

The next day, Ruggero says:

"Pelosetta, Pelosetta, bring Your Master his eggs."

"Right away, Your Majesty."

"You know, Pelosetta, last night I danced with a girl who was a beauty. She had a gown all covered in gold braid, shining earrings, and you should have seen her hair. But she stole my watch. If only I knew who she was!"

"Your Majesty should look for her."

Ruggero was bursting with rage. It passed. Another fifteen days went by and he says:

"Pelosetta, Pelosetta, you know, tonight I am going to another party."

"I hope Your Majesty enjoys himself."

He went, the trumpets blared. His old father Carlo the French king looked out from his balcony at the satin tent. He said: "But you are always going to parties! Is this how you intend to govern the kingdom?"

In the meantime, the fairy appeared. Pelosetta was amazed, and in her heart she felt tremulous ringing bells.

"Pelosetta, I am giving you a gown all covered in stars, shining stars, and earrings of gold and silver."

"O, what delight!"

The fairy dresses her. When she was ready, she set the horse flying through the dark air. The peasants were sleeping below in their houses. The weary half moon was rising with difficulty over the tops of the roofs.

"Look at her, look at her!" cried everyone, when they saw her arrive in the ballroom, alight like a day in the flowering spring.

Ruggero drew near to her. He gives her his hand. They start to dance a ring-dance, feet and hands intertwining. She manages to slip a ring off his finger. Making an excuse, she left. She flew off again on her horse through the wide bank made silver by the half moon.

When day came, the young man said:

"Pelosetta, Pelosetta, you know, that woman returned and this time she stole my ring with the royal seal."

"Your Majesty should be more watchful. Open those beautiful eyes. Here I am among the rooster and the hens."

So it passed. Another fifteen days went by, one after another, like beads of the holy rosary. Ruggero spoke:

"You know, Pelosetta, tonight I am going to a ball in the castle that belonged to our enemy King Frederick."

"Praise to you, my prince. Praise to God, Lord of the worlds and the celestial isles."

"Ha, ha," he laughed. "What language are you speaking?"

The young man departs, wearing a splendid helmet. Young Pelosetta leaves on the horse that mounts to the lofty heights, breaking open the gates of bronze. They arrive at the castle where Frederick once lived, gazing at the glittering sunsets of our village Minèo, gazing at the serried walls of the bare mountains. So...

Ruggero sees her, he invites her to dance. He thinks in his thoughts: "I must pay attention. I want to see what she is up to." While they were dancing a waltz that took one's heart away, she slips a gold chain off the Prince's jacket. He doesn't notice it. He noticed only when he got back to his royal chamber. "Oh, by Jesus our Lord, you can't win with her. Every time she thinks of something new."

When it was bright day, he said: "You know, Pelosetta, that girl robbed me of my gold chain."

"So then, she is stripping Your Majesty alive."

"If she were a man I would cleave her in two with my sword. You can't fight this sorceress witch. Who can she be?"

Then one day Ruggero had a desire for a sweet made with honey, cinnamon, and all the fragrant herbs of the kingdom.

"Pelosetta, Pelosetta, I want you to make me a cake with eggs from the birds in my garden."

In that garden there were sparrows, partridges, blackbirds, and birds of paradise.

"Yes, Sire." The girl hunted among the cinnamon and incense trees for the birds' nests all full with green, yellow, and red eggs. She worked them into a dough with her own very sweet hands, the dough under her fingers took whatever form she wished. She put her own thoughts into it.

From the top of the staircase she heard: "Pelosetta, Pelosetta, bring Your Master his cake."

"Your Majesty is served."

At the table, when the Queen Mother cut the cake, what does she feel? She touches something, feels it, then brings forth the ring without touching it.

"Where does this ring come from?" asked Prince Ruggero.

"How do you expect me to know that, master?"

"But this cake, didn't you make it?"

"Yes, but I don't know anything about the ring."

"What a crazy thing! What a crazy thing!"

So. It passed. A short time later, Ruggero, prince of the white eagle, said again to Pelosetta: "I have a great longing for another cake."

"May Your Majesty be served."

She mixed it: fragrant herbs, eggs of royal birds, the finest flour that she bought from Don Turì Casaccio, an excellent pastry-maker. When the Prince found in the cake the chain that made a dazzling light, he shouted: "There is the hand of some Saracen woman, an enemy of mine, in this. I will give the order to search out the Saracens who are still living in my lands. I will exterminate them."

It passed. After seven days, he again had the desire for a fragrant cake, and slicing it with his own hands, Ruggero the prince found inside the gold watch that in a perennial ticking beat out the substance of time. Ruggero shouted, and old King Carlo agreed: "Death to all Saracens!"

They were not aware that, in the meantime, tired of their

tormenting hunger, of the destruction of everything good and beautiful in the land of Sicily, all the people were in revolt against the King. One people, one river: they were killing the French who, filled with torment, with lifeless eyes, said not "Cicero" but "Sisero."

It was just as well that at a party – when Ruggero knew nothing of the enraged villager, the shoemaker in rebellion, the tailor shouting in the square, the potter turned arsonist – just as well that he discovered Pelosetta at a ball.

"It's me, my Master the Prince, don't you recognize me?"

She took the veil from her face, and her face shone like a summer's day.

He grew mad with love and said to his mother: "I want to marry Pelosetta."

"You want to marry Pelosetta, our servant girl?"

"Yes, Queen Mother. But have you seen her?"

"What do you mean, have I seen her? Always with her face blackened with ashes."

"Here she is."

"Is this Pelosetta? Can it be, my child, divine jewel?"

She was dressed in the gown braided with gold braid, her neck adorned with jewels. Her hair gave off black sparks, her voice was a song.

"O Jesus Our Crucified Lord, are you Pelosetta?"

Meanwhile the shouting populace gathered at the balcony. One carried a sword, another a gun, another a scythe, another a hoe, another the falcon with burning eyes that would tear out the heart of King Carlo.

"Stop, my people!" said the Queen. "My son Ruggero of the white eagle is marrying Pelosetta, a Saracen like you! Behold her!"

The people went wild. Pelosetta seemed to adorn the world with flowers. Everyone went to the temple where the sacristan said: "Children, time passes like a destructive river." There was the cobbler with his hammer and anvil, the mason Giovanni with his bucket and lime. There was Peppi the doorpost, and Turi the lame, and Matteu the oil vendor, and Cicciu the matchstick, and Ianu the greedy glutton, and Angiuzzu the chicory vendor. On wings, the sparrow, the lark, the green bird, the bird of paradise entered the temple.

The Saracen women, carrying couscous, incense, honey, and cinnamon, left the dim grottoes of the mountains. They left the dark alleys where their thoughts were formed, each one thinking in sadness. At first, all the women bent down to the ground, and their mouths kissed the earth where the worms of God travel, going from labyrinth to labyrinth. Then, giving thanks to God Macone, they played tambourines with their agile hands. They sang thus, to shame and to honor:

> *Tra la, tra la, tra lee,*
> *Seven Frenchmen for a penny;*
> *The penny's made of copper,*
> *Seven Frenchmen for a gutter;*
> *The gutter is full,*
> *Seven Frenchman for a bull;*
> *The bull has horns of ebony,*
> *Seven Frenchmen for our lady;*
> *Our lady is a Saracen,*
> *She's a diamond black and fine.*
> *Our lady is a roasted chestnut,*
> *Seven Frenchmen for a serpent;*
> *Our lady marries the French king*
> *who holds the kingdom of Peking;*
> *She wants peaches with sweet pits,*
> *Spindles, needles, bridles and bits,*
> *And the river runs to the sea.*
> *Tra la, tra la, tra lee,*
> *The Saracen is so enchanting,*
> *Seven Frenchmen for a pudding;*
> *The pudding tastes like gruel,*
> *Seven Frenchmen for a mule;*
> *The mule starts to kick,*

Seven Frenchmen for a stick;
Tra la, tra la, tra lee,
A Saracen is our lady,
Sweet and black and pretty.

As pleased God, as befitted the great Macone, the sorrow of the poor people was a burden. The burden became a lightness, the earth put forth leaves, on the mountaintops and in the rocks the birds sang.

Ruggero's leg is here, Pelosetta's is there, and we await the spindle, the shuttle, honey and bread.

The Child Mother

When the first cocks crowed and in the nearby countryside the farmers called to each other with the sound of a horn, I would still be in front of the oven with my father, Master Turi Casaccio, my sister Iana, and my mother. My father, who was a baker, had twenty-four children, and I was the last. Already at the age of nine I got up at midnight to help my father with his work. When he took the bread with all its different shapes out of the oven, the sweetness of the smell made me dream of the dawn that came over Minèo from the mountain district. Of course, at that time in our village there was no electricity and you had to go from one room to another with an oil lamp that sent out a red glow from its shade. Iano, our errand-boy, slept whenever he could, with his head leaning against the wall.

"Hey, Iano," my father would say to him, "this is no time to sleep. In a little while the shopkeepers in the square will be expecting their bread."

When the sun rose from the high scorched lands of Militello, I would run out. My mother would yell after me:

"Go to bed, Papé. You've been on your feet all night."

During those years we were staying in the house of the Barbèras, in the Santa Agrippina district. On the balconies, suspended from cane bars, you could see braids of garlic and azaroles. Seeing me, one of the women would say, "Where are you going at this hour, you wild pony of a Casaccio?"

I wanted to play, and since the streets were full of stones, I got the biggest one, dusted it off, and covered it with leaves and colored patches.

"Oh, what a big doll!" Angelina would say to me, or the Lombardo kid, looking for similar stones to imitate me. From on high, four or five miles up, the day was arriving. Who knows if, on the banks or on the shore, bushes weren't already starting to bud.

"Who wants to play with me?" I would say.

Farmer Peppi Titta, already very old, maybe a hundred years old, seated in front of his dwelling, would say to us:

"You're disturbing the morning with your shouting. Be still!"

"Hey, old man," I answered, "is it true that you're so old you have worms in your brain?"

"*Saecula saeculorum*," he said, getting angry, "I'll give you worms in your stomach."

I really was a terror. We would play with hazelnuts, using our fingers to press them into a dimple, and if I didn't win I would pull my playmates' hair. One time, there was a girl named Tatò, and I got her to use the hoe to take out all the stones that paved their stall. When the mule went in, those stones would shine. I had convinced Tatò that underneath them were veins of gold. Her father was a farmer, and when he got back from the fields that evening he wanted to kill her.

Anyway... The two Centamore sisters lived in our street, and since they were very old, they would ask me to do them little favors. But I didn't always want to do them. One time I poured salt into the two pitchers of water they kept in a corner (because there was no drinking water in those days in our village) and when they drank it they said, "How salty this water is! It must have been that rascal Papé Casaccio!" Another time I made a hole with a nail in their chamberpot, and at night when they made peepee they soaked the bed. One said to the other, "Are you blind? Don't you see that you're doing your business in the sheets?"

These Centamore sisters, to make me be good and still, would tell me, a little at a time, the stories they knew. They had learned these tales from their mother, Caterina, who had learned them from their grandmother, Giuseppina, and she from yet another grandmother. I managed to learn a hundred stories, and I told them to my playmates when the winter was harsh, or when we didn't have anything to eat except for the wind that entered our mouths through the cracks in our houses. I was born on March 6,

1894, and I wasn't even 10 years old when I heard these Saracen tales.

It wasn't always winter. But like I was saying at the beginning, when the mayflowers came out in jubilant bunches amidst the ashen clay outside the village, as soon as I turned out the bread loaves, I would go, with my big stone doll, through the turns of the alleys to the Salèmi Walls. Once I saw Maruzzedda, who was three years old. I grabbed her and ran with her in my arms to the flowering rock where there aren't any houses.

Her mother yelled after me, "Papé, bring me back my child. Where are you taking her, you devil of a Casaccio?!"

Those tall daisies of purplish yellow hid us out of the sight of anyone who might be looking for us. Around the two of us were bunches of small and large corollas that opened up in parallel layers at our passing.

Not much time went by before you could hear over the houses the voice of my sister Iana, who was six years older than me. She kept shouting:

"O Papé, where are you? Don't you know you have to bring the bread to the shopkeepers?" I didn't want to work anymore, when all through the riverbanks and the caves the day was unfolding in a whiteness of roses.

"O Papé, where are you?"

"Where are you?" the echo said. And again:

"-ou, -ou, -ou."

I urged on my playmates so I wouldn't be by myself. I would say, "Don't go to work in the fields with your mothers. We're children, and we should play." I managed to pull them along with me because I would tell so many stories. I knew them by heart in all their details. I knew when to raise my voice and when to lower it. I would look up at the sky, and in the course of the tales I would sing little songs and lullabies. Their mothers, when they saw me, wanted to kill me.

"Come here, you rotten Casaccio kid! I should eat up your soul! You're the one who leads away all our daughters with your stories.

Don't you know they're supposed to come to the fields to work?"

Sometimes I made up the stories myself. I amused myself the way a poet does, making away with sounds, words, shadows, taking the substance of life. That's how it was. I was a wild kid, I know.

Often I stayed by myself, and if I didn't want to carry the chest of bread into the square to the shopkeepers – you made a knife mark on a stick to keep track of the number of loaves – then I would go to find blind Don Enrico Amoroso.

I would find him seated at the top of the stairs, his body turned into fringes from the huge shadow that descended the stairs, in cross bars against the light. He would be waiting until, from some alley, mirrors set up deliberately would send him the rays of the sun to warm him up. I would go up the stairs on tiptoe so he wouldn't hear me. I would get behind his shoulders. I would see his blind eyes, and in one ear all of the sudden I would shout, "Hey, hey!"

"Oh, you wild kid, is that you?" he would say to me, his heart giving a start.

He would tell me to keep him company, seeing as his children weren't there, while he was waiting for the fragrance of the flowering valley to arrive on the breath of the wind.

"What's better than these smells, Papé?" he would say to me. "They're not roses, I know – there aren't any roses in our village – but delicate, fragrant, wandering vapors. Don't you ever chance to smell them?"

And in this way (while I, in my customary fashion, amused myself by throwing salt into jugs full of water) he would talk to me of:

> *rose gardens,*
> *of a thousand seeing eyes, all turned towards the moon,*
> *of saplings made of glass that gave forth light,*
> *of life that wanes with each passing day,*
> *of the fleeting waves of the sun.*

I would leave him only after, using a piece of glass, I had sent light his way, tangled up in the stones of the alley. And he: "Bless you, Papé, you warm my hands and my heart."

Then I would again pass by Don Peppi Titta who would sleep with his head down, with an earring in one ear that shone in cold points. I would go sit down on some step of the dwelling, with my stone doll in my arms, and rocking her in my heart and my arms, I would say, "Rest, my beautiful little baby, rest. The birds won't come to disturb you, and the lizards won't twist in the walls. You can see with your own eyes the glassy fragments of our lava, and God who comes with the wind. My life is not unlike yours."

She would go to sleep, she was really a rock in the language of our understanding. I would go steal basil just to perfume her all over her living person.

Then, tired, I again took up the path through those eternal stones, within the body of the shadows. My thoughts dissolved in the light.

Midday came, springing up over the village and passageways of the houses with countless peals of bells. When they began, there was a space of time between them. The loudest and most solemn was the bell of St. Agrippina. It filled the air in waves, which grew in geometric proportion, only to lessen its vibrations until they hurried off to die in the dust. I used to like to listen to the bells, standing with my face turned up so that the buzzing of the sound would cover my hair and forehead. When those bells became fainter in the valleys and on the mountains of Camùti, I would get close to the walls to hear the last broken vibrations. Anyway... I should mention that one of the women used to say to me:

"Are you trying to hear the spirits speak? Why are you disturbing them with your ear?"

There were tiny hummings in the stones that transmitted the sounds along internal lines. Even the shoots of certain hedges called *murari*o absorbed those drifting sounds, and murmurs garlanded the world.

Midday spread out over Minèo with the bells of San Pietro, Santa Maria, and the Capuchins. The first, between pauses, made the glowing things of the day even more delirious. The second, in a sonorous voice, after a brief expansion, was absorbed by the throbbing valley under the mountains of Arcura. The third rose from the Convent of the Josephite Capuchins, thrashed around in the sand caves, and suddenly rose to the heavens in all its strength. Then the hens, flocking together in corners in the shade, went to sleep with their feathers folded. You could again hear the worried voice of my sister Iana, "O Papé, where are you? where are you?"

I would return to the Salèmi Walls through tiny lanes where the sun was already making flames shoot up, and I would ask for some bread from one of the village women.

She would laugh, "Ha, ha, the daughter of the greatest bread baker in the world is asking me for bread. Ha, ha."

There was no one in the streets, and if I looked toward the countryside, I might happen to see some farmer who, at the spasmodic din of the bells, had leaned up against the trunk of an olive tree and gone to sleep. I would return to the heights, while I watched skylarks glittering in their careful circling flight.

"I'm not going home," I said to myself. "I won't even have time to sleep before I'll have to get up again to bake bread of semolina and the finest flour."

I would make necklaces out of mayflowers, adorning my black stone doll.

"Don't you like them?" I would ask her.

I wanted her to grow long, shining black hair, so that the kids in the neighboring villages would envy me.

"Just look at what a beautiful sparkling singing doll a little kid like her has got."

But, looking at the fields where the sun went along, filling even the tiniest holes in the olive trees, and the leaves of the almond trees, I grew sleepy. I would try to sing sad lullabies to distract myself, and I would say to the doll:

*My little girl, the one who gives you milk from her own
breasts truly loves you and does not deceive you.*

Some butterflies circled around me in the eye of love, and I would
say, "Go away, you're making me even sleepier."

Without realizing it, I would fall asleep. It seemed as though
flocks bleated in every part of the earth that in light and shade and
shadow gave strength and life to the countryside.

The thought would come to me: "Just look how they're making
fun of Papé Casaccio," as I felt within me a sleep like the bleating
of goats and silver sheep. My brother Giovanni would find me
asleep, and he would wake me up, saying, "Hey, you little rascal,
wake up. The grass has just about eaten you up."

And in fact, some tendril of ivy had wrapped round my hands
and some mayflowers gave life to my hair. There was a great
warmth in that den of wild growth, which was repeated in the
shining figures, and I seemed to see the olive trees of Fiumecaldo
that, like golden bushes, come sparkling towards me.

"Where are you off to?" my brother Giovanni was asking me. I
was off to the Centamore sisters, 83 and 84 years old, to have
them tell me the garlands of fables that now, having no longer the
divine loving memory of childhood, I am forgetting in my late old
age that comes like a winged charger and a rushing of birds in the
woods.

October 1978
September 1979

About the Author

GIUSEPPE BONAVIRI was born in 1924 in the hilltop town of Minèo in Sicily. Bonaviri began writing poems, stories, and novels before he was ten, and continued throughout his high-school and university years in the nearby town, Catania, provincial capital, where he studied medicine, receiving his degree in 1949.

After earning his degree, he began work on a novel. Having finished the novel in 1950, it ended up in the hands of Elio Vittorini who liked it a great deal and accepted it for publication in a series of new writers he was editing for Einaudi. *Il sarto della stradalunga* (1954) is the story of the author's childhood

He spent a number of years as a doctor in Minèo, some of that time at the Public Health Office. Bonaviri subsequently moved to the Ciociaria region, between Rome and Cassino, where he married in 1957.

After 1964, when he began private practice as a cardiologist in Frosinone, he was able to dedicate half of his time to writing. His works have been widely translated.

About the Translator

BARBARA DE MARCO was introduced to Giuseppe Bonaviri during a lecture tour that brought him to the University of California, Berkeley, in the company of Giovanni Bussino, who had just published his own translation of Bonaviri's *Notti sull'Altura* (*Nights on the Heights*). Invited to choose from among Bonaviri's many works, she became captivated with the *Novelle Saracene,* which appealed primarily to her medievalist appreciation of the interplay between folklore and miracle tales.

The encounter with Bonaviri also came at a time when the translator was investigating the traces of Arab language and culture in medieval Sicily, an interest she continues to pursue through historical and hagiographical works.

Bordighera Press

presents

Crossings
An Intersection of Cultures

A refereed series, CROSSINGS is dedicated to the publication of bilingual editions of creative works from Italian to English. Open to all genres, translators are invited to send detailed proposals.

Contact: Anthony J. Tamburri, Bordighera Press, John D. Calandra Italian American Institute, 25 W 43rd St, 17th Fl, NY, NY 10036; anthony.tamburri@qc.cuny.edu